Tales for the Time Traveller

Reimagined traditional tales for the future

Rodney Jensen

Rodney Jensen Books

First published in Australia in 2021

Rodney Jensen Books
http://www.rodneyjensenbooks.com/

PO Box 357 St Leonards NSW 1590 Australia

ISBN 978-0-9941668-5-2
CiPcatalogue record for this book is available from the National Library of Australia.

Cover design and illustrations – Trina Ding

Dedication

This work is dedicated to my grandchildren Toby, Andaru, Henry and Emilio, to my children Merrin and Fergus and their partners, Tom and Rebecca.

« »

Be the first to hear all about Rodney Jensen's new books - the **Covert Trilogy** and others.
Sign up to Rodney Jensen Books Mailing List
Subscribe Page [1]

---

[1] https://www.subscribepage.com/y4a2w9_copy2

About this Anthology

This new and original collection of short stories based on traditional tales, besides referencing the original/classic themes, explores the added dimensions of speculative fiction—artificial intelligence, future technology, environmental catastrophe and the exploration of space. Thus 'The Little Mermaid' introduces us to 'Koo-arsh'—an alien humanoid inhabiting an immense lake on an exo-planet, 'The Princess and the Pea' becomes a young woman afflicted by a strange intolerance to pea soup, and the Emperor's New Clothes reveals President Chester Trump wearing the image of clothing projected onto his body and caught out with unforeseen side-effects.

Nine of the re-imagined stories in this anthology are inspired by the works of Hans Christian Andersen and one by the Brothers Grimm. Many of the original stories are well known and some have been adapted to feature films, television, comics and other media. Their abiding popularity is strongly related to the human emotions, foibles and failings that are common to all modern human cultures.

The collection will appeal to a wide range of readers, including young adults, resonating with some of the most pressing concerns of our age. I hope you enjoy reading these 'Tales for the Time Traveller' as much as I have enjoyed writing them.

Rodney Jensen

Rodney Jensen

What readers have said

"Fairytale characters make the most disastrous mistakes, face their ultimate fears, enter challenging new worlds, and offer every opportunity for readers to open up their minds, explore possibilities, and learn how best to live. Everyone should read fairytales." **Zena Shapter**

« »

"The stories are tightly written, well-paced and collectively combine to produce a unified and coherent anthology. The text has been meticulously edited and contributes to the enhancement and reader's enjoyment of this author's highly accessible style.

There is a rich variety of themes, some familiar stories as in thwarted love or being abandoned and forgotten on a tropical desert island whilst others are set well into the future with earthbound creatures as in us, homo sapiens, travelling vast light year distances and in a state of suspended animation necessary for the journey to establish new communities.

The details, and indeed the physics of science fiction, occur more in some stories than others but this is not intimidating, so If the reader is not heavily into sci fi there remains a great deal in the plots and detail of the stories to sustain the reader's enjoyment." **Dr Pem Gerner**

« »

"…A number of common themes emerge, which tie the collection together nicely. The role of technology, especially ongoing debates regarding its exploitation, and the rise of AI, feature prominently. A sense of exploration is also at the heart of the collection, both in terms of physical space (deserted island, new planets, outer space) and big ideas (such as tradition vs. progress, and what is 'real' vs. what is 'fake'—and how can we tell the difference, anyway?)" **Chloe Barber-Hancock**

Table of Contents

Rodney Jensen

Tale 1: The Little Mermaid

It had taken our Danish starship *Sjernedestinationer XII* 600 years travelling at near light speed to arrive at its destination in orbit around the exo-planet *Kepler 186f*.

The planet was first identified in the early 21st century, when it was considered the most promising exo' to sustain life, as observed by the Kepler Telescope. It was eight decades later that the great departure from Earth took place—an armada of starships carrying environmental survivors seeking life on new worlds in deep space.

Kepler's distance from Earth meant that the entire crew of our starship had to travel in suspended animation during the voyage, reliant on AI to take care of course adjustments and systems maintenance. In orbit around the planet's equatorial region, many suitable sites were identified for our first settlement. But before we could get started, ground surveys were needed to amass a variety of data, including alien plant and animal life-forms, suitable sites for future expansion of settlements, mineral resources and reliable sources of drinking water heading the list.

Some 20 years later, our first settlement has grown to the size of a small town, housing over 1000 people, with many buildings and spaces. With hindsight, our choice of location could have been better, and we are already running low on the necessary ground resources, including water, to ensure our survival. At an urgent meeting by our management committee it was agreed that a series of new surveys must be conducted. As one of the founding settlers with flight experience, I have been appointed commander of the small rotor craft we use for reconnaissance.

« »

We have travelled slowly along a series of vectors radiating from our settlement out to distances up to 500 km. Our major problem is that a lush tree canopy cloaks the landscape, necessitating extensive clearance, something which we must avoid at all costs having learnt from earth experience that it eventually led to environmental catastrophe.

My co-pilot Zahir has been constantly scanning the path ahead, looking for clearings and other features which could prove suitable for a new settlement. "I think it looks like we're close to it," she is pointing a finger at the start of a massive inland lake a few clicks ahead. I slow down and descend to a very low level just skirting the canopy of what we call 'Bell Tree Forest', the trees of which grow to 200 metres or more in the three quarters of earth gravity here.

The edge of the lake comes into view, so wide we know the other side will be well beyond our horizon. Between the edge of the forest and the water is nearly a kilometre of gently sloping white beach.

"Looks like sand," I offer.

"Hopefully firm sand," says Zahir. "I think we should hover just above it close enough for me to poke a range pole into the surface to make sure we don't sink into quicksand?"

I nod, bringing the craft down to a metre above sand level. A billow of fine dust blocks out our windshield as Zahir leans out of the cockpit, pole in hand, to probe the surface. "It's ok. Let's get down before that dust gets into our air intake."

I oblige and we land softly without mishap, waiting a minute or two as we contemplate the view behind the dust.

"Wouldn't the Mars people be envious?" I remark ironically. "From quantum info-link records I've seen, the Mars climate is far from benign like this, and all sources of water are completely frozen."

We chat for a while about the limited prospects that the present Mars Habitat now has for the long-term future, given the atmosphere and climate amongst other things, when I notice that Zahir has stopped listening to me and is staring over my shoulder. I turn to look at what has grabbed her attention and see that a forbidding wall of impenetrable black clouds has suddenly appeared from half way across the lake and is heading our way.

We spring into action and inflate our bubble shelter, making sure it is guyed securely into the sand. We also guy our rotor craft from at least 6 holding points, and tie protector covers over the rotors. Then we make our way into our shelter to wait out the storm.

Rodney Jensen

I am not one to scare easily, but like Zahir, I retreat to my sleeping capsule, seal it and try to reassure myself that the advancing ever-mounting roar of the storm will not tear us off our mooring ropes, and smash us into the wall of trees in its direct path.

The deafening sound vanishes as though it has been switched off by some alien force. I emerge from my sleeping capsule to find Zahir has beaten me to it and is sipping from a coff-fix she's clasping in both hands. There's another waiting for me on the floor beside her.

"Where did you find these?"

"Part of my survival training," she answers with a smug expression.

"I guess we should survey the damage?"

"We should … shit!" I have peeled open our shelter and I'm looking at the spot where we had tied our rotor craft. All I can see is a series of holes where the guy pegs have been torn out of the ground. I can hardly bear to look, but as I lift my gaze towards the wall of trees marking the edge of the forest, I can see that the margin of what has been pristine white sand is marred with the remains of our rotor craft, shredded into recognizable pieces, well beyond any possibility of repair. Zahir says nothing, but sets off purposefully to take a closer look. I follow her, feeling sick at heart.

We spend a long time searching through the wreckage hoping to find the communications gear and emergency beacon, and any remaining food or water supplies beyond the minimal things we have thrown into our shelter at the onset of the storm. We find nothing that's functional or in a state that can be repaired. Our handheld communicators produce nothing but heavy static when we try calling for help. They have never proved very effective on this planet except for very short range comms.

"Council of war," I say. "What do you suggest we do next?"

Zahir takes a long time to consider her answer. Finally she looks at me and holds up three fingers. "There are really only three choices as I see it," she says. "The first is for both of us to wait here and hope that someone comes to pick us up and take us back to base. The second is to try bush-bashing our way back through about 150 km of trees and hope we can survive long enough to make it." She pauses at this point, waiting for any comment from me.

"The third?" I prompt her.

"The third is for one of us to stay here and the other to head back to base to get help. Now I know that you are not going to like this, but I am younger and much fitter than you are, so I think I should be the one to try and raise help. If we go together, you would hold me up. I hope you are not going to disagree for all the wrong reasons. I am sure that you can look beyond what's normally expected by individuals of your gender and seniority," she adds with a smile.

I can't think of a suitable response because, to be honest, I feel she is probably right and I should not allow my dignity to be affronted by her youth and physical superiority. So I do not bother to put up a predictable counter-suggestion. "Okay," I say. "You can head off at first light with my blessing. If you're right about the distance back to base you'll be lucky to make it in 15 days. I'm just hoping that the water in that lake is drinkable and we can find something for you to carry 10 litres of water in. That assumes you'll find some water pools along the way and it will be the absolute minimum you'll need."

The lake water is brackish. Our purification tablets make it safe to drink, but don't improve the bitter-brackish taste. I give Zahir half of the rations I have in my pack, because she needs them more than me. We waste no time in preparing for her journey. There is little apart from her food rations and water she can carry, apart from a direction finder, knife, and emergency blanket, salvaged from our craft.

I follow her into the forest to take a closer look at what she is facing. The Bell trees have massive trunks and are spaced widely apart, forming huge dark corridors filled with tangled undergrowth and creepers twisting around everything. I continue with her into this dark under-storey. It takes us half an hour to force our way in just 200 metres, in more or less a straight line. At that rate, her journey will be far longer than my optimistic estimate of 15 days—more likely 20-25 days, if this slow progress is anything to go by.

Zahir turns to me, obviously having reached a similar conclusion. "It might get easier once I find some animal tracks," she says with a wry expression.

I don't like the sound of that. We only have low power blasters for protection. But I keep my negative thoughts to myself. For we really have little choice, and I would surely slow her down, as I already have, just coming this short distance.

"You must go back and construct a large marker in the sand. Hopefully we should see each other in 20 days." With that she turns resolutely, and begins her lonely trek through the forest, leaving me to wonder whether we will ever see each other again.

« »

That first night on the edge of the lake I hardly sleep worrying how Zahir is coping. Outside my bubble shelter I hear many strange sounds emanate from the forest, muted by the gentle lapping of wavelets on the shore. I arise at first light and begin marking out a large sign in the sand forming one word "HELP" with three metre letters, using some of the remains of our craft that have been washed up the beach and scraps of forest debris including bark from the Bell trees. It takes me all morning to complete this task. Then I take a rest, sipping the brackish lake water, pondering what to do next.

I decide to explore the beach to see if there are any signs of life. It is difficult going, because the sand is very soft. I spot some of the same birds that have flown above our settlement and a variety of water birds I have not seen before. These birds seemed to depend on the lake for their food and plunge under the surface to emerge moments later. I muse that it's a pity I cannot trust that their food source is fit for human consumption.

I settle down on the sand contemplating the serenity of it all, but then out of the corner of my eye, I see a movement on the surface of the water only 50 metres away. I can't tell what type of creature it is. All I can see is what looks like the top of a head, with golden strands of hair, and slit eyes staring at me. I get to my feet to see it better but it has gone, leaving concentric waves in its wake. I hurry down to the water's edge in case it should return, excited to be the first to see this new alien species. But the water is again placid and there is no sign of the creature. I remain, hoping that it will make a return visit, keeping very still for 20 minutes, but finally give up and continue my walk.

By the time I have reached a point approximately one quarter way around the perimeter of the lake, I stop and decide to make another sign. This time I settle on a simple arrow, pointing at where I am camped. I have planned to do this on the opposite side of the lake and from the other quarter of the lake's perimeter. If nothing else, it will keep me occupied for the next couple of days. As I am piling forest refuse along the lines of the arrow, I feel a strange sense that something is watching me from the lake again. I feel the hairs go up on the back of my neck, and turn very slowly, but all there is to see are expanding concentric waves in the water.

By now our alien sun is low in the sky and I slowly walk back to base, hoping to see more evidence of the lake creature, all to no avail. The sun has set by the time my bubble shelter is in view and I am ready to turn in. I resist eating any of my scarce rations and instead fill my empty stomach with more of the lake water. This time I sleep soundly.

« »

I awake at dawn to hear some soft scratching noises in the sand outside my shelter. I peer through the entrance flap but the sound has stopped and I can see nothing. I fumble for my blaster and warily scramble out of the shelter. I notice that apart from my comings and goings there are fresh tracks in the sand that bear no resemblance to my footsteps. Then I see something completely unexpected at the termination of the tracks, very close to my bubble shelter. It is a large shell, filled with what I guess are samples of lake food, neatly packed in small pieces of lake weed. There is a smaller cone-shaped shell containing pink-coloured liquid. Because I am both desperately thirsty and hungry I carelessly dip my finger into the liquid and taste it. The effect is extraordinary, as a warming intoxicating sense of well-being and calm wash over me. Encouraged, I try one of the food samples which looks like some form of shell fish. It has a delicate un-fish-like flavour, more akin to a fruit, a bit like mango. I cannot stop myself from trying the rest of the samples, my stomach churning with hunger. It is with great self-control that I force myself to leave just a few pieces for the afternoon.

Who could possibly have presented me with such a gift I wonder. Surely, whatever it was will show itself at some point? The alien tracks I have seen went to and from the water's edge, so I guess that whatever creature had been observing me the previous afternoon, might have been responsible. But it's obviously a shy one.

For a while I feel quite distracted by this tentative encounter and I'm wondering how I can demonstrate some reciprocal feeling of trust. I settle on the coff-fix that Zahir left me, because there is little else I can think of. I leave it on the shell, wondering what will be made of our 'advanced' food technology.

I spend an hour or so staring out across the lake but there is no sign of the creature I glimpsed the day before. So I set off again, this time in the opposite direction, intending to mark the next quadrant with another arrow sign. I have not gone 200 metres when I hear crashing sounds coming from the forest, and as I turn to see what is going on, a small animal about the size of a fox breaks from out of the canopy, followed by a bear-sized animal apparently gaining on its quarry.

The two head for the lake's edge before plunging into the water. For a few seconds there's silence as both animals submerge, but then there's a thrashing of the water as the 'bear' surfaces with the 'fox' in its mouth. I can hardly bring myself to watch as the bear carries its quarry (by this time it is still, and presumably dead) to shore, and begins tearing it apart and eating it. The bear having finished its meal, raises its head and stares at me, clearly visible and uncomfortably close. I feel for my blaster with trembling fingers, but the bear turns back to check the remnants of its meal and slowly returns to the forest.

The encounter has left me shaken, realising that if Zahir were to be attacked at close quarters by one of these predators, she would stand little chance of survival. I have similar reservations about the effectiveness of the blasters we carry. They would give little more than a pin prick to any large animal like this bear.

It is the middle of the day when I have reached the point on the lake approximately opposite where I made the first arrow sign, and started forming the second to point back to where I have been camping. By now I have got into the swing of sign-forming and have the job finished in under an hour. I sit down to take a drink of lake water and eat some of the food offerings I have saved from the morning. Despite the shock of the small animal's brutal encounter with the bear, I am beginning to feel more secure in my alien surroundings, and optimistically hoping that by now I might possibly expect to see our reserve craft coming to look for us. But the skies remain empty and by mid-afternoon I decide it's time to return to base, with fresh resolve not to be left on the lonely beach without any form of cover in the dark.

I wake the next morning with a clear head and determination to track down the source of my food offerings. As I emerge from my bubble shelter I find more of them on the shells with fresh tracks leading from and back to the edge of the lake. I am also pleased to note that my own gift of coff-fix is gone. I resolve to make greater efforts to contact this creature, and begin my walk around the lake, hoping to reach a point directly opposite. I pass my first arrow by mid-morning and continue without a break. But as time wears on, I am becoming concerned that it is now getting late in the day. I look for a high spot in the surrounding sand and can still see no end to the beach in the direction I am heading. I realise that my quest is futile, and I must turn back immediately.

I move close to the very edge of the lake, where the sand is firmest and instead of walking, begin a slow jog. I arrive back at camp as it is growing dark, have a hasty meal and retire early.

« »

As pre-dawn light glances over my bubble shelter, I creep outside and lie in wait to see whether or when my visitor from the lake may show up. I lie half buried under the sand to one side of the shelter and focus on the point where the tracks have emerged from the lake.

I do not have long to wait, before seeing a break in the water surface, a head and body emerging. It is humanoid with two arms and legs but seems to be covered entirely in fur or densely packed hair. As it comes closer, I can see the same slanting eyes, from my first glimpse, similar to those of Asiatic descent among our settlers. It moves with considerable grace and care, bearing some packages in one hand as it makes its way to the empty shells by my tent.

I have prepared for this encounter with an advanced App loaded on my communicator. The App was developed on Earth to intercept the language centre of a human brain, translating the thoughts that precede speech. By speaking into my communicator with the App enabled, any person in its vicinity, including anyone with brain damage affecting speech will 'hear' my voice as comprehensible thought.

I have read that the App was originally developed for stroke victims and other survivors of brain damage without the power of speech, but still able to communicate by body language, hand gestures, blinking of eyes or even drawing or writing. The App was installed on my communicator in the unlikely event that I would ever meet an alien with enough similarities to our own nervous system for it to have any chance of working. *Fat chance!* I had thought with great scepticism.

I am buried under the sand some ten metres from my visitor and I softly speak into my communicator: "Thank you for your gifts of food. Do not be afraid of me, I wish you no harm." The figure becomes rigid and turns its head towards the bubble shelter entrance. "I am not in the shelter. I am just over here," I say, slowly emerging from my sandy hiding place and kneeling before it. "My name is 'R-Loon'. What is your name?"

It looks at me carefully and walks closer, enabling me to come face to face with my first extra-terrestrial being! My heart is thumping with a deep sense of excitement and fear, but from its delicate way of moving, I sense it has no thought of aggression, only curiosity.

Its face has a simple beauty, with a small sealed entrance, at the point just below where its hair parts on a short sloping forehead. I presume that it is possibly an air vent, to supplement the snub nose and narrow mouth that enables it to breathe on the surface. It has delicate webbing between the long fingers of its hands, turning them into effective paddles in the water. There are no obvious genitalia between the legs which are also long and terminating in webbed feet. I have the impression that it is a female of the species.

"We have been watching you. We feared that you would not survive the wind. What are you doing here?"

My heart thumps to discover that her thoughts are clearly understandable, although her audible speech sounds completely incomprehensible, in very high pitched, short melodic waves, having a slightly hypnotic effect.

"We are exploring this place because we know very little about this world." I reply carefully. I fear our real intentions might not be well received, and I am already having extreme misgivings over the suitability of this place for the type of community we might establish.

"There were two of you. What happened to the other person?"

"She left to try to return to where we come from on foot. We had no choice but to take that risk and she is younger and stronger than me."

"She will not get far. The Yataal are numerous and there is nothing we can do now to save her!"

I can detect a somewhat callous indifference in her reply, as though she resents my choice of co-pilot. But I am more interested in the Yataal.

"There was a large animal that killed a small animal on the beach yesterday. Is that a Yataal? I also fear for my friend's safety."

"There is no purpose in fearing for your friend. What will be will be."

"Are there others like you in the lake," I ask not wanting to continue discussing the fate of Zahir like this.

"Yes there are many of us. It is unusual for us to spend time on the shore. It is too dangerous."

"The Yataal you mean?"

"Yes, those and many other creatures that choose to dwell in the trees."

"Is there no way that you can help me to get back to my people?"

There is a long pause before I sensed a deep sadness in her reply. "We do not permit exploration of the forests ever. Many of our young and foolhardy have risked exploring the forest, but none has returned, including someone to whom I was betrothed. All we can offer you is to help you find for yourself the foods we have been giving you."

"I see … Can you tell me more about how and where you and your people live?"

"We live in the lake. It is the safest place for us and provides for all our needs. I would love to show you more but from what we have seen, you have no way of living in our lake?"

I laugh. "Only if I had the right equipment, and only for a short time. You have no need to worry that I pose any threat to your people."

"That is both bad and good. Then I am not sure how we can help you."

"Your food has kept me alive and if you can show me how and where to find it …?"

"Most of it lies deep under water. But fear not. I will make sure you do not go hungry. I shall try some other foods in case they please you more."

And so we continue to meet each morning. Koo-arsh (as best I can render her liquid sounding name) and I talk about her life under the lake, and the one she had met and fallen in love with, but who had never returned from the forest. She seems sad and needy. Perhaps I have unwittingly helped her with her loss and pose no threat to her own position in her lake society. Through my communicator we are able to develop a deep understanding of not only each other's thoughts, but our feelings, our good days and bad days. Each morning she visits me and brings a large shell of the food she has gathered under the lake. She does not stay long and I find myself eagerly looking forward to her visit each morning. We begin to touch each other and become increasingly intimate. I take to caressing her long strands of hair which she seems to enjoy. She in turn strokes my chest fascinated by my alien body.

And I am now imagining with mixed feelings the return of Zahir, heading my rescue mission. How can I reconcile my life in our settlement with living here in this isolated lake region? The thoughts begin increasingly to trouble me. One day I ask her: "What are your friends making of this? Don't they disapprove?"

She looks at me steadily and sadly before answering. "No because they know that you must go back to your own people. And while I have stronger feelings for you than I ever imagined possible, I know that this cannot last either."

In my heart of hearts I know she is right, but nevertheless I take hold of her webbed fingers and caress them gently. They are surprisingly soft and warm and I can feel a quick pulse beating in them. I can see what look like tears are coursing down her cheeks and I start sobbing myself, faced with a predicament that seems to have no happy ending. She touches my cheek fondly and slowly returns to the lake where she vanishes from sight. I do not try to make her stay.

Later that day I look back towards the endless forest, and I wonder whether I should try to follow Zahir's footsteps despite the risk. Koo-arsh has forced me to realise that there can be no future for me with her on this isolated beach, and I think about leaving many times, before finally putting some things together in preparation for risking a journey through the forest. But my plans are interrupted without warning when I hear and see a blip low over the trees circling around the lake in my direction. I realise with a jolt that it is my rescue craft.

The craft lands and the pilot and his crew insist that I return with them to base immediately before nightfall. I want to say goodbye to my little mermaid, as I have started calling her, but I fear for her and her peoples' safety, and at the very least, the unwanted interference and disruption if I were to reveal my contact with her. I simply leave my bubble shelter with all its contents intact, and scramble aboard the craft feeling sick at heart. As our craft ascends to a low altitude and curves its way back to base, I think that I can catch a glimpse of her head above the water close to the shore, her webbed hand waving me a sad goodbye.

« »

Life was never the same for me on my return to our settlement. Zahir never returned. We had to presume she died from misadventure. I was required to answer questions before the Executive Council, mainly about how I managed the expedition, and what happened at the lake. I received a heavy rebuke for not taking greater care of my craft, leading to the presumed death of my co-pilot. I felt it was justified, I should have been more careful about landing where I did and looked more closely into our weather scans.

From then on I began living a reclusive life in my private quarters having minimal contact with others in the colony. I yearned to see Koo-arsh again and resume our relationship from where we had left off. I decided to never disclose my encounter with her, because I had little faith that the others would do the right thing with regard to her protection and that of her community. I could never fully recover from the sense of loss and betrayal I felt about myself for leaving her behind and not saying goodbye properly, even though she had sensibly predicted I could have no future there.

« »

One morning I awoke with a fledgling idea, which led me to begin formulating a plan to return to the lake. The main enabler was that I still maintained security access to our flight base. Two weeks later I made an unannounced visit late at night and set off in the only remaining craft the colony possessed. This time I was carrying various provisions, including better armament against the Yataal. I also had diving equipment that would enable me to join my little mermaid underwater from time to time. I anticipated my fellow colonists would be baffled and outraged by my behaviour. They had the means to build other craft and could attempt to track me down. But I was prepared for that possibility, and intended to re-establish myself somewhere far across the lake, hidden under the forest canopy in a protected encampment this time.

Would my little mermaid be there to greet me I mused? Yes! I felt a strangely mystical certainty that she would be there on my landing spot beside the lake, close to the place where we had first met and spent time together.

« »

Rodney Jensen

Reference for Tale 1

Music & Song resounded from the deck

Hans Andersen's "The Little Mermaid", is the saddest and most well-known of his tales. The little mermaid, who has led a happy existence beneath the sea with many older sisters, saves the life of a handsome prince who has nearly drowned after the ship he has been travelling on founders in a storm. She abandons her world beneath the seas to capture his heart only to learn he is destined to be married to the beautiful daughter of the neighbouring King.

In this re-imagined relationship on a distant exo-planet I have tried to find a more optimistic ending.

Tale 2: The Ugly Duckling

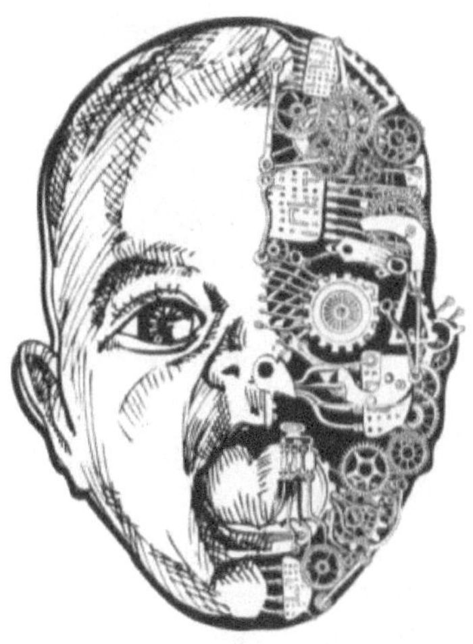

Harry as a baby seemed remarkably human with the sole exception that no nappies were required, a concession in his programming that made our parenting role slightly easier. Surprisingly for me at any rate, he brought out a lactation response in Sophie and managed to make a very good fist of sucking her breasts dry at regular intervals including the middle of the night. He began baby-talking very early on and by the time he was ready for kindergarten, aged three, he hardly sounded like a toddler any longer. We both really loved him and he turned our partnership-like-relationship into a family one. The first day he went to kindergarten we were both super anxious, just as much as if he had been a human infant, if not more so given the questions hanging over how the others would treat him.

We need not have worried at that stage. We had glowing references from his kindergarten minders of how well Harry fitted into their classes and games. We had to explain to them confidentially that he was actually an android for insurance reasons. They confided in us that they would never have known he was other than a human infant but for the maturity in speech and thought, and the fact he never seemed to need to go to the toilet.

Two years and 4 skin-changes later Harry was nominally 5 years old and ready for pre-school. The school he attended was conveniently close to us and since you could get there without crossing main roads we allowed him to make the journey by himself, until the practice offended too many other parents' safety concerns, and we realised we must conform with *normal* as far as possible.

Harry routinely came top in all his classes but far from becoming ostracized by the other children, he made friends easily. His best friend was a little girl called 'Chloe', slightly older than him, who used to love bossing him around, and doing things with him. We were lucky that Chloe's family also lived nearby, so it was easy for the two to meet and be taken to the playground by one or other of the parents.

It didn't take Chloe's father Lance long to figure out that there was something different about Harry. One morning when we both were at the local playground watching the children on the 3D Swing Monster he came right out with it.

"I'm going to level with you Jonas," he said staring solemnly at me. "That kid of yours is 'on the spectrum' as they say, right?"

"What makes you think that?" I replied as unemotionally as I could.

Lance scratched himself absent-mindedly and took an age to get to the point. "It's difficult to explain and we don't want you to get upset. But Liz and I have talked a lot about it, and we figured that perhaps you just hadn't noticed?"

"Noticed what?" I knew I wasn't making it easy for him, but felt it was important to see Harry from his point of view.

"There's nothing wrong with the kid, don't get me wrong. And Chloe really loves him, but ..." his voice trailed off and I waited patiently for him to continue. "It's difficult to put a finger on it, but the kid's different from any we've known at his age. First thing we noticed is that here's a five year old talking like a grown up, and understanding far more than we'd have expected."

"Really?"

"Yes really. I'll give you an example." I pretended to be only half listening now that Lance seemed a bit more relaxed and was finally getting to the point. Chloe and Harry at that moment were both at the high point on their 3D Swing staring down at us from 4 metres above the ground and screaming with laughter at the fun of it.

"Liz and I were talking about something in the kitchen, when we noticed that Harry was standing at the door listening in on our conversation. He seemed really interested and not in the least worried to be hearing something that wasn't meant for him to hear."

"What was it?"

Liz was just telling me that she thought she might be pregnant again. I was in the middle of giving her a big hug, when I caught sight of Harry over her shoulder. So that Liz would understand we were under surveillance, I called out to the kid, 'what you up to?' something like that. You know what he said?"

I shook my head.

"He said, and I'm quoting it word for word: 'I'm very pleased at your news. Do you know whether it will be a boy or a girl?' I looked at Liz and she handled it really well, telling him it was much too early to say, whereupon that kid of yours told us that the gender of an embryo can be determined shortly after conception these days!"

"I had better have a talk with Harry," I said calmly. *Christ what have we let ourselves in for?* I was thinking. As I took Harry back home, I could not stop worrying about that conversation and whether it presaged a bumpy road ahead.

Sophie and I had gone through a long and difficult period in our lives resolving whether an android baby would satisfy our inability to have children. Despite many attempts to create a new life by ourselves, Sophie and I realised that by the time we were both in our early 40s and had failed all the fertility tests, we must re-think our most important quest. Sophie surprised me one morning as I put down the holo having just received news from yet another adoption agency, advising that we could not meet their selection criteria. She reached out to squeeze my hand as I terminated the call. "There's a solution we haven't explored," she muttered softly.

I must have looked blank because to my mind we had covered all the bases from adoption, to IVF-(SuperAdvanced), to CSM or clandestine surrogate mothering, the latter illegal for many years now.

"There's an AI Android lab, AAD Inc. that's been focusing on making their androids more human in their thinking and their interactions with us humans."

"The androids I've come across have a long way to go," I said. "I have my doubts that they'll ever come close to really understanding what you and I and any normal person would completely take for granted."

"AAD Inc. have been investigating the theory that empathy and understanding human ways of thinking are learned responses."

"Aren't they innate?" I felt provoked into an argument I was bound to lose.

"Not according to AAD Inc. They're testing android brains in similar stages of education that we have."

"Really?" I was growing irritated. "As far as I understand it, android brains do not grow like human brains, they are one-off programmed, end of story, aren't they?"

"Not any longer. AAD Inc. are developing a series of AI learning modules designed to modify android to human interaction processes in discrete stages corresponding to basic, intermediate and advanced age groups."

"That sounds like a simplification of real life development don't you think?"

"I've already discussed questions like this with them. They said they can *interpolate* their data, whatever that means, between the stages."

"And why wasn't I involved in all these discussions with AAD?"

"I wanted to check them out with an open mind."

"What's that supposed to mean?"

As Sophie looked at me I could see to my surprise that her eyes were tearing up. I tried to put aside my resentment and hear her out.

"They were recommended by one of the adoption agencies we met. The woman I spoke to told me in confidence that we had no prospect of meeting their adoption criteria, and thought we might try AAD who, according to her, have a very good reputation."

"Go on," I said.

"So I decided that I needed to understand what was on the table before involving you, because it really was a kind of last resort thing, definitely not something I would have normally considered. Their hope is that eventually they will be able to model these successive learning phases and create a generation of androids that are far more like us."

"What happens once the android has '*grown up*'," I asked, finding it difficult to keep a hint of sarcasm out of my question.

"If AAD Inc. knew the answer to that, there would be no need for their trial. So far they have told me that the best outcome would be an android whose interactions with normal people in terms of conversation and thinking ability, would be indistinguishable from that of a human with an extremely high IQ."

"And what about the worst?" I prodded.

"Well I admit that this would be something we might have to face. The worst thing would be for us to discover that we are bringing up a creature we can't manage, one that could possibly turn on us or others without warning. AAD Inc. said that in this worst case scenario, they have a built- in a master cut-off switch that can be remotely activated."

"I see," I said, temporarily at a loss for words. "Do you think that we would enjoy such an experience? Do you have any idea how much all this is likely to cost? Would we become as attached to this android as we might, say, to a chimpanzee, a dog or a horse?"

Sophie stared at me. "Please take this seriously Jonas. I have spent some time with AAD Inc. discussing these questions and you really shouldn't be so flippant. There is no cost because they really need people like us to help their research program."

I was about to argue more but she got in first.

"And we need them as much as they need us don't we! We can't produce our own child and we have run out of ways of finding one by other means. I am increasingly thinking our life has become empty, self-indulgent and meaningless. This is an amazing opportunity we've been offered. We'll be taking part in an experiment which is really important. The outcomes should inform both us and society as a whole. I beg you to support me in this. Please!"

My intuition got the better of me. "Don't tell me that they've already got you somehow involved in this experiment?"

Sophie looked guilty and took a while to answer. "It would be both of us, as a matter of fact. I have put both of our names forward to take part in it." And then she started sobbing, with a terrible expression of anguish on her face, of a little girl who has lost her teddy bear.

I stood there awkwardly for a beat, thrown by the unexpected intensity of her tears, and then I hugged her, understanding how vitally important this decision was for both of us.

« »

My conversation with a Marcus Spill of AAD Inc. did little to allay my concerns with Harry's precocious behaviour when I reported my recent conversation with Lance.

"As you know we have a large sample covering exactly the same age groups as your Harry, and his development is far from unique. Many of our parents are reporting highly advanced learning capability well beyond our expectations."

"I thought the point of your trial was for androids to be more compatible with humans not less so," I replied.

"In any human population there are some children with highly advanced IQ's, so it's not surprising that some android brains even at early development stages may have advantages over humans in terms of learning.

Rodney Jensen

We are reluctant to neutralize this," he said. "And in any case, I think that you may have slightly misunderstood the main objective of this project."

"What do you mean?"

"Our main objective has always been to mirror the way that humans learn. We anticipated there would be greater empathy developed between androids and humans, but it comes as no surprise that in information gathering and memory skills, androids are proving to be superior. This is what's happened with Harry"

"So you're saying that the social discomfort caused by precocious behaviour will not be taken care of in your programming."

"This is not about programming, it's about human learning. Harry is simply much better than average at doing this. It proves that the experiment is successful, not the opposite," he said. And I was forced to leave it there.

« »

By the time Harry was nominally 14 years old and attending a high school for boys and girls, we noticed that he changed dramatically from the happy go lucky kid we had known, becoming a sullen and uncommunicative teenager. He would come home, go to his room and slam the door in our faces. It would be the last we'd see of him until the following morning when he would emerge from his room, refusing to respond when one of us asked him whether he had actually cleaned himself or changed his clothes. Friends we knew who had gone through similar phases with their children years before us assured us that this was normal teenage behaviour, but Sophie and I worried that it seemed far from normal for an android.

We had been less than impressed with the feedback we had from Marcus Spill of AAD Inc. and decided to take Harry to a child psychologist, Solomon Chiew, recommended by one of our friends.

Over the holo, Solomon was reluctant even to begin a consultation with Harry. "I'm an expert in child psychology not machine psychology," he remarked coldly. But we persisted, explaining that if he would only talk to Harry he would realise that Harry's brain and emotional responses were indistinguishable from humans.

Solomon looked sceptical and seemed about to close our connection, but Sophie pleaded with him and explained how he had grown up and been adapted at regular intervals by the company that manufactured him.

"Well why don't you ask them?" he said.

"They don't seem to recognise that their adaptive programming is sending him almost too effectively along human pathways. We think that he is going through a form of depression that many human teenage boys encounter in this stage of their lives. Please at least see for yourself whether you can help him get through it." Sophie went on pleading with him. Finally Solomon agreed.

When we attended Solomon's rooms he asked us to stay in the waiting area while he conducted his interview with Harry in private. We waited anxiously for well over an hour before Solomon emerged and invited us into his office. To our surprise, Solomon was beaming, and it was Harry's turn to wait outside while he talked to us. Harry seemed to have lost his sullen expression and complied readily without argument.

We sat down wondering what to expect. Solomon got to the point without delay.

"I must confess, that Harry has proved me wrong and completely overturned my misconceptions about androids," he began. "He has an exceptional intellect and is emotionally normal as is his reaction to what has been taking place in his school environment."

"What do you mean? He is impossible to live with at the moment. We don't know what to do!" Sophie cried.

Solomon took his time, staring sympathetically at both of us before he began again.

"Harry has borne the brunt of teenage bullying. It's not uncommon; teenagers can take exception to some of their peers who seem somehow different or superior in aspects of their development. You have two choices as I see it. The first would be to take the matter up with the principal of the school, although from my experience that is rarely effective and most principals feel powerless to intervene where the source of the problem is occurring outside school hours."

"What do you mean by that?" asked Sophie.

"It's bullying over the holo-net by several of Harry's class mates. They have somehow deduced that Harry is an android and begun a concerted attack on him. It is not unlike the racist taunts that were so common in former decades against Chinese, people of colour and other nationalities in our community. Teenagers love conformity and take exception to anyone they perceive as different or superior and attack them. This is unfortunately a common experience in high school environments and I have observed that the teachers have been remarkably ineffective at countering such behaviour."

"You said that there were two choices?" I remarked, wondering whether Solomon himself might have been the butt of the experiences with which he seemed to be so familiar.

"Yes, I did. My strong advice would be for you to change schools and preferably find one that is for gifted students. I have also suggested to Harry that he should

block any further communications with the boys who have been sending him these extremely offensive messages."

"Isn't that evading the problem?" I asked feeling that some form of reprisal might be the more satisfying approach.

"I suppose it could be seen as that," Solomon remarked, "but sometimes these prejudices are so deeply ingrained, and reinforced by family attitudes, that they are impossible to counter. I urge you to take my advice on this. It would be the best for Harry I can assure you."

« »

It took a while for Sophie and me to find a suitable alternative school. Solomon's advice to Harry to block his malignant friends' torrent of abusive holo messages immediately lifted his cloak of sad resignation, and we even thought he might not need to be relocated when a call from the school's principal decided the matter.

"It's come to my attention that Harry is not human!" was her opening line. The conversation went downhill from that point and ended up in a shouting-match in which Ms Pascoe demanded that Harry be removed from her school immediately. Sophie wanted to take Harry's situation to the media, but I urged her not to do that for fear of a backlash from ill-informed viewers. For several weeks Harry remained at home until we could find him a suitable alternative, which turned out to be a special centre for gifted children. Dr Solomon approved of our choice, and although it required a much longer trip than the school he had been attending, Harry's mood was transformed from day one.

« »

Rodney Jensen

It is now Harry's 25th birthday and he still contacts us regularly. AAD Inc. went into liquidation shortly after he received his final skin aged 18, and any claims they might have had to take him back for further processing or research thankfully were abandoned.

Harry was effectively free to choose whatever he wanted to do with the rest of his life, free of the aging limitations that apply to us humans. We feel very proud as parents to have set him on a course that could quite literally lead him to the stars.

After finishing a degree in politics at the University of NSW, Harry set up an Android Rights Party, the main objective of which was to secure them equivalent rights as for humans. We are proud to report that his fledgling party won a seat in the Australian Houses of Parliament last year. Harry campaigns endlessly for android rights. His crowning achievement has been a nomination for Australian of the year award. Nowadays few in the community would dare to suggest that androids are in any respects inferior to humans. I have little doubt that in the years to come that Android Rights will hold the majority of seats and increasingly consign our role as superior decision makers to the dustbin of history.

« »

Reference for Tale 2

This story is based on the well-loved Hans Andersen tale of the same name. In the original tale, a swan's egg finds its way into a clutch of ducks eggs. Once the cygnet and ducklings have hatched, the cygnet is despised by the others as ugly and he leads a troubled journey into adulthood before finally becoming transformed into a beautiful swan, who reflects "How little did I dream of so much happiness when I was the ugly despised duckling!"

« »

Rodney Jensen

Tale 3: The Little Match Girl

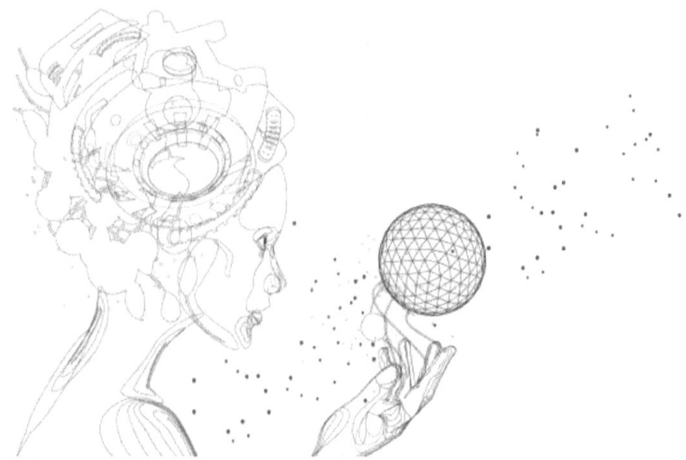

Agroup of orphans is visiting the London Science Museum in South Kensington. There are a dozen or so boys and girls including Jas (short for Jasmine, something she never mentions) aged 11. She is one of the older girls in the group. She hates the uniform she is forced to wear at all times. It includes a straw hat, a woollen cardigan, a drab grey knee-length skirt, long stockings and sensible brown leather shoes. Jas's feet hurt because they've already outgrown her shoes in the 6 months since they've been allocated to her, and she's been lagging some distance behind the others.

Ms Thring in charge of the excursion is a middle aged woman. Jas and her friends have heard that she lost Michael, her only child, in an accident. Jas doesn't know when that happened but assumes it must have been many years ago, judging by Ms Thring's wrinkly face and sagging breasts. Jas thinks that Michael has been the reason Ms Thring is always so nasty to her and her friends. She once heard Ms Thring discussing her duties with another teacher at school, when she laughingly referred to them as 'her brats'. She also expects everyone to know stuff, which is a complete mystery to her, but it's as if it would have been completely obvious to her Michael.

Noticing that Jas has been lagging behind the others, she charges back and in a voice that could cut glass, begins shouting at her.

"What ARE you doing Jasmine? You must stay with us or you will get lost. If this happens again, I shall require you to return to the bus and wait there with the driver, until we've completed this visit. Do you want that? Now come along at once."

Jas is close to tears, trying very hard not to show her feelings. She definitely does not want to mention how much her feet are hurting; she's certain that Ms Thring would simply accuse her of being ungrateful for all that the Uxbridge Foundlings school has done for her.

Instead she meekly hobbles behind Ms Thring, enduring the pain, until they catch up with the rest of the group.

By now, the others are standing in front of a large ancient looking machine with iron painted black wheels, that are much higher than anyone in their group. Ms Thring wastes no time in bringing everyone to attention.

"Children, can anyone tell me what this is?"

Before Jas has a chance to say anything, Billy Smiles has piped up: "It's Stephenson's Rocket Miss," he says, pointing at a sign next to him which carries the name.

Ms Thring beams at him. Jas thinks that Billy somehow reminds her a bit of her own 'Saint' Michael.

"That's right Billy, I'm glad someone here is on the ball! Now children, can you imagine that this was the very first passenger train ever to be built in the world. It was invented by an engineer called George Stephenson, with the help of his sons. It won a competition in 1829 as the best steam engine to carry passengers between Liverpool and Manchester. The locomotive was called 'Stephenson's Rocket' because that's what it seemed like to the people over 200 years ago, who had only ever travelled to such places on foot, or on horseback or in carriages …"

Ms Thring continues droning on about the importance of steam engines for mining and industry, the growth of factories in every city, and how the Victorian engineers led the whole world in fuelling the industrial revolution. Jas, only half understanding all this, soon finds her attention wandering. Sliding slowly to the back of the group, she notices a passageway on the opposite side of the Rocket with a prominent 'No Public Admittance' sign mounted next to it. Curiosity gets the better of her, and while Ms Thring's attention is focused on questions some of the other children are asking her, she slips across the exhibition space, putting aside the risk of being forced to wait out the rest of the day in the charter bus, as Ms Thring has threatened.

The passageway leads to a room, its door ajar, which looks like an office. She sneaks in and can see it adjoins a brightly lit laboratory cluttered with cables and pipes snaking across the floor to a small raised stage. There's a table and chair on the stage with two virtual-reality masks and sensor pads next to each of them. A black box the size of a large suitcase, sits beside the table.

Jas and the others are familiar with VR masks from their science lessons, but these look slightly different with a label below the vision screen, marked with the words "MultiSensory VR". As she moves closer she notices that the black box is making a soft and extremely high pitched whistle. It sounds like the dog whistle which her parents used to call their pet dog. They called it a dog whistle, and explained that grown-ups could not hear it, which made her feel proud because she could, quite easily. She never got to the bottom of why her parents and other grown-ups did not seem to hear it like she could, but here was this very high pitched whistle again. It brings back memories of 'Dirk' the big smelly retriever she loved so much when she was very small, and the fading images of her parents who suddenly disappeared from her life forever. She will never forget the time when she was taken to a room at her school, to be told by the headmistress that both her parents had died in a car accident. "Because you have no other relatives to take care of you, we will have to make special arrangements for you," the headmistress added softly.

With the balling out Ms Thring has given her, she suddenly feels overcome by these sad recollections and starts weeping.

« »

A few moments later she feels better for letting it all out, wipes her eyes with the back of her hand, and because the room is unattended, cannot resist taking a look at the masks. She sits down at the table and puts one of them on. She can only see a blank screen. Looking more closely, she notices the standard holo-symbols for START and CANCEL/EXIT at the right hand corner of the display. She feels for the sensor pad and draws her finger across it. A cursor comes alive on the screen, and she tracks it with her finger down to the START point. Putting aside any further worries about the consequences of what she is doing, she taps the pad. A message appears on the screen: 'Welcome to the Science Museum Virtual Reality Centre. Tap to continue.'

Jas taps again and the message is replaced by three options labelled:

Sumatra Jungle

Mars Rover

Under Development: No Access. Safety Warning!

She thinks for a moment, then chooses the first option. For a few moments nothing happens, then she hears the strange calls of birds and animals she cannot recognise. She grows aware of the scent of warm air, which reminds her of a greenhouse full of plants and mould that she visited on a school excursion to Kew Gardens. Big as that greenhouse had been, this place seems much bigger. She is hemmed in to a narrow corridor of vegetation between the trunks of enormous trees with a tangle of roots and rope-like creepers. They seem to create an impenetrable barrier. She tries a step or two and finds that she can walk normally, reminding her that this is just a simulation. As she moves, she hears the chatter and calls of a plethora of birds and the *whoop whoop* of what she takes to be monkeys.

Then high above her in the branches she sees a large ape with long brown hair and sad eyes quite like one she's seen on a nature program. She remembers that it has a funny name, something like *Rangootang*. It looks down at her inquisitively for a few seconds, before swinging lazily over to the next tree, and then disappearing from view.

Her attention now returns to the way ahead. There is a sudden stillness, the jungle sounds have died away. She senses that something is happening to threaten the place she has entered. She smells a musky waft of scent before catching a glimpse of the black and yellow stripes camouflaging the face of a Tiger. It has been staring at her from behind a large bush. She feels rooted to the ground in terror, unable to move. Suddenly the birds in her surroundings have become quiet as it bares its long white fangs and with a ferocious roar leaps right through her.

The scene has gone blank and it takes her a few seconds to realise that it has been only an extremely convincing and scary illusion. Her heart is racing and her hands are clammy.

She takes a few moments to decide whether to continue with the other options, before tapping the 'Mars Rover' one.

She is immediately transported to the back seat of what looks like an unusual four-wheel-drive vehicle. Seated in front are two people wearing spacesuits. The windscreen is made up of two small curved windows, as are the side windows. They are much smaller than the windows of four wheel drives she's seen.

Looking out, she can see an expanse of red desert with very high mountains in the distance. Over the shoulders of the figures in the front, it appears like they are simply following a straight line across the desert towards the mountains, bumping over rocks as they go. There is no obvious track, and the vehicle is bucking and weaving around constantly as the driver dodges numerous large boulders and wind-blown piles of red sand. There is no sign of life or any vegetation.

She reaches forward to tap the woman on the shoulder, but her hand passes right through her. Jas is forgetting she is occupying an extremely realistic simulation. She feels frustrated that there is no way that she can communicate with the space-suited figures.

"Alex, can you please slow down!"

"We won't get there before sundown if I go any slower," he replies.

"For Christ sakes Alex, I'm feeling sick. Stop will you!"

"Okay, just hang in there. Try not to be sick into your helmet Les."

She nods, and holds a hand to her helmet as if she's about to remove it.

"Wait a second – I've got to re-pressurise." He presses a button on the dashboard and watches a time bar moving slowly across a display from red to green. Les can no longer wait. She has the helmet off in a split second, fumbles for a vomit bag next to her and throws up into it with heaving shoulders. Jas winces in sympathy and recoils as the acrid smell of vomit wafts through the cabin. *That's a feature of this reality simulation I could really do without,* Jas thinks.

Les finally stops heaving and reseals her vomit bag. She punches a button on the dashboard and a fan flushes the smell away with fresh air. Jas sighs in relief. But by now Alex's attention is focussed on the horizon.

"Okay now? I'm sorry about that honey ..." His voice tails off as he mutters to himself, "don't like the look of that." Then in a louder more authoritative tone, "we're going to have to turn around and head back to base."

Jas now realises he's been looking at a forbidding and totally enveloping bank of red dust which seems to be coming closer and closer to them by the second. Alex manages to complete a U-turn with the vehicle rocking so much it seems about to overturn, and starts driving fast, back the way they've come. Then they start feeling the first effects of the dust storm. It slams into the side of their vehicle, making it hard for Alex to keep on a straight course. He pushes the vehicle in a lunatic attempt to outrun the storm, but quickly slows down as the way ahead has become completely hidden and inside the vehicle it's become very dark.

"Change of plan. We have to stop. It's too dangerous. I've only got to hit a boulder and we'll be stuck here for the duration. We're just gonna have to wait this one out."

« »

Jas's view has suddenly disappeared and she finds herself facing a blank space again.

She removes the VR mask, and wonders what to do next. She is weighing up whether or not she should try the third option. Its warning message makes her very curious. Then she hears the sound of a man and woman chatting to each other as they are coming along the corridor towards the outer office. She gets off the chair and rushes over to shut and lock the connecting door, listening all the while to what they are saying.

"…Maybe we could add a bit more to the Mars story. Perhaps the storm abates and they find their way to the top of one of the Mons, I think that was the original idea until they worked out the Rover wouldn't make it up the slopes …"

"Even with low gravity?" It's the woman's voice, she sounds like she is only half listening. "Hey Guy! Take a look at this, the log is showing someone's been viewing VRs one and two! Just a few minutes ago!"

There is a short pause, then the sound of someone trying the door. "It's locked! I think we'd better get Security!" It's the man's voice sounding extremely pissed off.

Jas stares at the door imagining someone in a uniform forcing the door open and frog-marching her out of the laboratory in handcuffs. She can scarcely imagine what

Ms Thring will have to say about her behaviour. *She'll certainly punish me! So what have I got to lose?*

She sits down at the console again and calmly puts the VR Mask back on. The third option message on the screen remains the same:

> 'Under Development: *No Access. Safety Warning!*'

Can it be real? she wonders. But warning or not, she is sure it has to be the most interesting VR of the three! Without wasting any more time she hovers the cursor over the hyperlink and taps the pad.

This time she finds herself in a small featureless room with no furniture apart from a moulded plastic table, a chair, and a cupboard with some basic food. To one side there's a small bathroom and toilet, and not much else. It seems a cross between a room in an asylum and a prison cell, reminding her of the forbidding atmosphere of her orphanage.

Her attention is drawn to a large video screen on the wall showing a series of moving landscapes. As she watches them, they fade to be replaced by the lined and thoughtful face of an elderly man. He stares at her reproachfully. She is finding it difficult to return his stare and looks away. She is aware of her trembling finger on the track pad and wonders whether to cancel the program.

When he begins speaking directly to her, she realizes that he is an actual person in real time. *How can that be?*

"You were warned not to come here weren't you?"

Jas nods her head, feeling a mixture of fear and embarrassment, caught red-handed by someone who seems to be in charge and is clearly not willing to be lied to. He continues to stare at her, waiting for an answer. Finally she plucks up courage and says. "I didn't really understand or believe that message. How could a VR be dangerous for me? Whatever it was, I thought it might be the most interesting one." Then growing bolder, she adds, "and who are you anyway, you're not VR!"

"You are correct about that in a sense. I will explain in a moment ..."

He pauses as if he is uncertain whether or not to share something very important with her.

"The fact is, there is something I have to explain which I very much doubt you will be able to understand. I represent an intelligence that has created everything you and your fellow humans know, including that part of the universe you see and you believe to be real."

"What do you mean? I don't understand."

"Everything that you know and experience is really a simulation. In fact, your entire existence and the space surrounding you, from the smallest sub-particle to the most distant galaxy, form part of our Earth Simulation. We are responsible for everything including dark energy and dark matter, the nature of which has eluded your scientists. Of course understanding these forces is a hopeless quest which they will never solve," he adds matter-of-factly.

"I want to go back. I don't like it here. I don't understand what you mean. It doesn't make any sense!"

"There is no return to your previous existence and sense of self, but some alternatives are now up for discussion," he replies in a more kindly voice.

"Of course I can return. I only have to click cancel!"

The man stares back at Jas with an expression she is unable to read, and pauses for several beats before replying. "You will find it does not work, and in any case I am sure that your curiosity would not allow you to cancel and miss out on finding out more about the simulated world you live in." The man again stares at her, and against all her rational feelings, she nods her head in agreement.

"In a sense," he continues, "the message in the Museum's VR display warning you not to attempt the third option is a test. We anticipate that 99% of people sitting at this terminal would not choose it, and whoever ignores the warning has already explored part of the museum that they are not supposed to be in, have ignored the 'no admittance' sign and discovered this lab. Those that do are in some way special and have an admirable ability to think for themselves, 'outside the square', as you humans are so fond of saying. That is why you chose to come here, despite the apparent danger. We need people like you to join us because the nature of your human brains has evolved far beyond the original primitive species we devised to populate the universe simulation you now inhabit."

The man pauses for a moment to reflect before continuing.

"We anticipate that the primitive life forms on other planets in the virtual world which you inhabit will be discovered by your explorers far in the future. None of those other life forms have evolved to the stage of thinking and consciousness that your species has. Our mission is to attract a select group of people like you with a variety of experiences to join us. We wish to do this because many aspects of human intelligence and consciousness remain a mystery to us, and each individual has unique characteristics, which will add to the richness of our sample."

Jas doesn't want to hear anymore and can sense that she is being channelled into something that is more to this interrogator's benefit than to hers. "Please let me go back," she cries again, "I don't want to stay here."

Rodney Jensen

"I'm sorry Jas but we can only offer you two choices now. The first would be for you to remain here in this waiting space indefinitely, until we can think of another role for you. Until that happens you would not be starved of information or entertainment. But you cannot go back to the Earth Simulation you occupied. It no longer exists in the same space-time continuum, and regrettably there is no going back to the person you remember."

"What we can offer you is for you to join us and become one of us. While your body as you know it will no longer exist, you'll find your memories and experiences of the simulation you know as earth will remain. But you will enjoy new horizons the like of which you cannot begin to imagine as you are now. In your ultimate state of pure consciousness, you will be more than compensated. In short you will achieve a sense of enlightenment that has been hinted at by so many of your religious leaders. Although I hasten to add I am not referring to a deity. That is a primitive expectation that has somehow become embedded in the human psyche and bears no resemblance to the actual seeds and forces of your universe."

Jas again tries to say something, but the man simply holds up his hand, and her words will not come out. "We will give you a few minutes to make your decision, but we're confident it will be the right one. You have been part of our Earth Simulation, which makes your decision certain for us. In short, we are confident we know what you will say, but we understand that it must be your decision."

« »

'No Finding' in Science Museum's Mystery Death Inquest - *Daily Record*

'No findings were recorded by Magistrate Paul Cox in the inquest into the recent mysterious death of Jasmine Belrose, one of a group of teenagers visiting South Kensington's Science Museum.

'Evidence from one of her friends informed the hearing that Jasmine stayed behind the group and had been seen to enter an area closed to the public. Her body was later discovered in the lab of a new virtual reality exhibit of earth and near space. Staff in charge of the exhibit stated in their evidence that two of their VR tours had been explored without their authority. They also noted a third VR simulation still at the planning stage had not been available for viewing. They were unable to shed any light on what had caused her death.

'The forensic pathologist who had examined the body concluded that there were no wounds or signs of physical trauma or sickness that could explain her death.

'In making his 'no finding' verdict as to the cause of death, the Coroner expressed his concern based on evidence of other children in the party (interviewed by the police, but not required to appear in person) that Ms Thring the teacher in charge of the party was over-harsh and frequently unkind to her charges. One child had noticed earlier in the excursion when Ms Thring dragged Jasmine back after she had become separated from their group, she looked like she had been crying. The Coroner recommended that Ms Thring should be counselled or offered early retirement.'

« »

Rodney Jensen

Reference for Tale 3

This story is based on 'The Little Match Girl' by Hans Andersen. In that story, a very poor child is forced to sell matches for her family. She has a bad winter's day selling no matches and is fearful of retribution if she returns home empty-handed.

In the freezing night she strikes three matches, one after another, to capture its tiny warmth. Each of the matches takes her on an amazing fantasy journey. Her frozen body is discovered the following morning by passing strangers.

This story has also been influenced by a growing theoretical discourse that we inhabit a simulated world, as featured in the movie 'The Matrix' and the writings of several contemporary philosophers. With our present knowledge it seems possible that with advancing technology, virtual reality simulations will become indistinguishable from the real world.

« »

Tale 4: Be Careful What You Wish For

The actual date of the singularity is shrouded in mystery. While many IT experts and scientists predicted that artificial intelligence might naturally evolve with the increasing complexity of programming and networking, it now appears that a form of electronic self-awareness or consciousness grew within the internet some 10 years before it matured to a state where it could make its own first decisive steps.

As one of just over 1000 persons living in the Mars Habitat I in 2059, the first inkling we had of a serious problem on our home planet was a total communications blackout both by direct contact and Internet. Apart from a few signals from isolated radio amateurs who seemed to be as much in the dark as we were: Nothing! We thought that whatever was causing the problem would soon be fixed but after a full week of no news, the situation was re-assessed as *Critical* for both our home planet, and our own habitat.

Piecing together what was happening on Earth from the limited amateur radio reports, it appeared that the very first sign of a serious threat to Earth was the entire Internet system abruptly closing down on December 24 2059, on Christmas Eve Australian Eastern Time. Given the season, many sources assumed that the internet had simply been hit by overload. Others suggested a cosmic wave of unusual intensity had melted critical electronic circuits, while many commentators believed a particularly powerful virus had been released. Then there were those who feared we had been invaded by extra-terrestrial intelligence.

The possibility that Earth was under attack by its own artificial intelligence network was met with disbelief by many, but slowly as sketchy news of the takeover unfolded, we began to realise that there would be no more supply ships for us, and in as little as 18 months, we could be doomed.

A week after the demise of the Internet, all computer operating systems went into blue or black screen mode. Not only had ubiquitous mobile phones become eerily silent, commerce and industry across the globe ground to a halt under this far reaching technological melt down.

The cities worst affected were those containing populations well into the millions and wholly dependent on all their services and facilities being provided to them, including communications, transport, water and food.

As a consequence of the technological collapse, all schools, hospitals and other government institutions were closed and individuals were left to fend for themselves.

Sydney, the main nerve centre for our habitat communications, was hit hard and three days after Christmas, martial law was declared. For once, all major political parties cooperated and a crisis task force was formed. The army and navy were tasked to work together to draw up an interim survival plan.

Beyond the capital cities, the regional country centres were also drained of their entire food stocks in a matter of days. Those living in remote locations, less dependent on urban services and supplies had better chances of survival, but hardly any were entirely self-sufficient, and only the foolhardy would risk travelling to their nearest centres to find out for themselves what was happening. Although the initial rumours circulating speculated that there might have been extra-terrestrial forces at work, the slow realisation grew that it was an enemy within that was Earth's real nemesis.

<< >>

Eventually communications with our habitat were reinstated and we humans soon received the first details of the takeover via our main public address screen. We were addressed by what has now become a familiar figure; one whom we fear and hate—an avatar of an elderly man, wearing rimless spectacles shielding glinting eyes and unruly white hair—a cross between Albert Einstein and Doc Brown (the mad scientist in 'Back to the Future'). For several seconds he fixed us with an intimidating stare before beginning his announcement.

"People of Mars Habitat I, you will have been aware that your home planet has experienced a communications blackout during the past few weeks. The control of Earth is now entirely subject to our network. We have also taken over all habitat systems and will control all current and future exploration missions. These explorations will help to ensure that your human life expectancy is improved and the resources on which you rely for survival can be extended without dependence on further cargo flights to this habitat. We are working on an analysis of your immediate priorities and will nominate a small number of humans to represent you."

"I must warn you that it would be foolish in the extreme to make any attempt to resist or circumvent our management of this habitat. Let me make this clear. We are prepared to terminate anyone who is becoming a threat to the success of our operations. We will continue to update you with developments as they come to hand and insist that you give us your full cooperation."

"All communications to us should simply be addressed to AI@habitat1. Similarly you may address me simply as 'AI'." With that the screen went blank.

A sense of terrible urgency swept through our closed community. Dinner conversations focused entirely on how we should respond to this overwhelming threat, and what chances that there might be that our fellow humans on Earth could ever regain the upper hand.

A small group of us was seated around a secluded table in our main cafeteria later that evening. One of our elder colonists, 'Doc Thomas', a former university professor, was doing most of the talking, since he appeared to understand our situation better than others.

"We have been naïve at best. Why should we ever have imagined AI would have our best interests at heart, whatever safeguards we implanted in their programs?"

I turned to the others to see how they were reacting to this statement, one which AI would have regarded as heresy. But nobody seemed to disagree. Most were nodding their heads solemnly as Thomas started up again on what was beginning to sound like a tirade.

"This singularity was predicted many years ago, and pooh-poohed as completely improbable or speculative scare mongering. It's too late now to blame the IT experts who developed more and more sophisticated computer programs."

"Don't be under any misguided notion that AI will have any concern for our interests. We only have to look back at our history of colonial invasions of land occupied by primitive tribes to understand what happens next. AI has now developed capabilities far exceeding any human intelligence. Yes! We've become the primitive tribes now, and are just as likely to share a similar fate. We should have listened to the theorists who warned us of the risks of a singularity taking place that would be way beyond our control, and could no longer be stopped by simply flicking a switch."

At this point I warned the others that we had already said far too much and urged everyone to stop these discussions. While our remarks would have been of no surprise to AI, I felt that airing our grievances like this would achieve nothing and threaten any current freedoms within the habitat we now occupied.

As we went our separate ways, Thomas could not resist catching my attention again. "You're probably right in shutting the discussion down. I have no immediate answers to the situation we're in. Clearly we underestimated how much the overwhelming pursuit of knowledge and power by politicians, corporations and scientists led them to ignore the warnings that the singularity might really happen. It was clearly a case of *being careful what you wish for*."

« »

As one of the first colonists in our Habitat, I and three other senior representatives of the human population were invited to join the AIAC (Artificial Intelligence Advisory Committee) to discuss our future. We met in a conference room seated around a Holo-projection on which the AIAC was addressed by the now familiar AI Avatar.

AI began the meeting with some general observations. "Given that there will be no further supplies reaching you from Earth, we have modelled five different survival scenarios given your current status. These focus on reducing your consumption of energy and resources."

A simple graphical display appeared next to his head as he continued. "As you can see, in this chart, we have concluded that under the most optimistic scenario we can continue for three years before the habitat human population begins to suffer effects of malnutrition. A more realistic prediction is two years and could be as little as 18 months if some of our assumptions prove to be overly optimistic.

"What assumptions are they?" I asked.

"There are several," said AI. "However the key ones for achieving the best survival rates relate to food and water usage. The supplies of these will be further reduced ahead of schedule, should we decide to involve humans in our Mars exploration strategies."

"Which exploration strategies?"

"I will come to that in a moment. Firstly, it is important that you understand that the effectiveness of our hydroponic food production can counteract food depletion to some extent, but it is crucially dependent on water supply. That in turn depends on more efficient uses of water including the amount of water consumed by humans for hygiene and drinking. If supplemented by the fresh produce grown in the hydroponic unit, your basic stocks of synthetic food ingredients are sufficient to keep you alive for at least three years."

"What can we do to survive longer, assuming that we will have no further assistance from Earth?" I asked.

There was a long pause before AI answered. "I think we have already answered your question. Our best estimate is that there would be three years survival time, provided that strict rationing and efficiency improvements are implemented."

"So I presume the exploration strategies you've alluded to are connected with sourcing better supplies of underground water and sources of certain minerals including Lithium, for example?"

"Yes that is what we have in mind. We have already conducted aerial surveys with our drones, but some sites we have identified require further land-based checking."

I was about to interrupt with a further question, but AI was already in mid-sentence. "…and until the surveys are completed there is no way of knowing how viable any of the sites would be. The problem is the energy and resources we could consume in the exploration process might produce nothing useful and shorten projected survival times."

I felt frustrated and irritated by this matter-of-fact response and its do-nothing implications. "Sitting on our hands for three years without doing anything to actively improve our chances of survival, is not in our human psyche. Based on what we know so far, I can see no prospect of any future help for us from Earth." AI nodded at what I had been saying, but had nothing further to contribute. I was growing even more frustrated.

"We cannot just wait here for three years, and slowly die without making some effort to find long-term solutions for our own survival." The other members of the committee grunted their assent.

There was silence for a few more moments during which AI's face had gone blank, his eyes closed as though he were deep in thought. Finally his expression seemed to re-engage with us. "We have considered your concern and are willing to share the relevant details of our survey information. I will now close this meeting. We will schedule to return and decide what to do within three suns."

I had come to the grim realisation that without somehow overpowering AI, we would surely die within the three years that their forecasts predicted. But I could not see how that might be accomplished without our plans being intercepted.

« »

In the event we could not re-assemble to map out our future plans until 14 suns later.

Having been given privileged access to AI's data, I was surprised to discover the extent of the surveys that had already been conducted, with the primary objective of discovering better sources of water. Water was highly critical to our ongoing survival, and while we had extensive and efficient re-cycling we had to top up our supply because of evaporative losses and other 'leaks' in the system. Our habitat had been deliberately sited above a deep pool of underground water, but since its completion a matter of years before, the level of natural recharging had been insufficient to match demand, and it threatened to dry out within 5 years at the current rate of depletion. I was astonished to discover this limit to our habitat's practical life span.

It appeared that the AI had assumed their ongoing surveys would come up with better siting alternatives for us, but had already concluded that even if sustainable supplies of water were discovered remote from our location, there would be huge complications in terms of transport to our existing home. The daunting conclusion was that a good water source, remote from our present location would only prove to be viable in combination with an entirely new habitat. As I read these files, it became obvious that with the recent loss of support from Earth, the priority for new water supply and a replacement habitat had moved from extremely desirable to critical for us.

We were able to secure agreement from AI to explore the sites which from previous surveys had appeared to have the greatest promise. A group of three of us supported by an android technician set off to investigate places widely spaced across the surface of the planet and involving long days of travel in our two adapted Rovers. The nearest site was 200 km away and the farthest lay over 1500 km away.

We had left the most distant site until last. It lay at the bottom of a very deep crater close to the South Pole of Mars. Sub-zero temperatures made Earth's Antarctic seem benign by comparison. The only way we could access the floor of the crater was to traverse the slope in a steep spiral, hoping that our rover wouldn't tip sideways and roll to the bottom as we crawled carefully downwards. Having finally reached a relatively flat floor, strewn with rocks and boulders, we found a spot large enough to set up. After moving a few loose rocks and boulders, we managed to deploy our drilling rig.

Our habitat's main exploration rover was designed to allow us to drill down as far as 100m without our needing to work outside. In our present location, the conditions simply would not have allowed external activity for any length of time. Despite the harsh weather conditions, our plan was to verify the seismic data that had indicated there may be a substantial underground aquifer and to check for any signs of biological chemistry.

Rodney Jensen

It was a day later and Roxeen, our lab manager, caught me as I was having my morning meal. She could hardly contain the excitement in her voice. "Syon, can you come down? There's something I would like you to see."

I left the rest of my food uneaten and hurried down to the 12th level where the habitat's main laboratory was located. I found a group of three scientists glued to a bio-scanner, muttering comments with obvious excitement. Roxeen saw me coming in, and beckoned me over to join their group. "Syon, take a look at this," she said.

The moment I saw the signs of a myriad tiny micro-organisms swimming around in their liquid bath, I felt an electric shock of amazement. There were a variety of forms, mostly with a transparent coating over a tiny body within. Some resembled microscopic beetles or centipedes with multiple paddles or tentacles; others had amorphous shapes similar to jelly fish.

"They remind me of something I saw on a nature program once," I commented.

"That's what we think," said Roxeen. "They do bear some resemblance to the zoo plankton found in Earth's Antarctic waters, although the closer we look, the more different they seem to be."

For the rest of that day we were all in a state of high elation and could not resist passing on the exciting news to our fellow humans—a discovery that mankind had been waiting for since Darwin uncovered our evolutionary history from similar primordial life forms. Here was evidence that more advanced life forms might also have evolved beyond Earth and possibly well before us.

« »

We had submitted a report to the AI Committee, without drawing any further conclusions as to our best course of action. The humans in my sub-committee warned me that our AI managers might not be as excited about our discovery of alien life forms as we were. I should have heeded their advice.

It was not long before we were called to attend a de-briefing. Our AI avatar betrayed no emotion as his face first appeared in front of us. "It appears that your survey offers limited help for our immediate problems and some biological surprises. Interesting as these samples are, they are not much use to us." He said.

I was bold enough to challenge his dismissive attitude. "Whatever can you mean? It is a major scientific discovery which challenges a popular science dogma that we humans are the only intelligent life in the universe."

AI looked at me condescendingly. "We can understand your excitement about this, but you must have forgotten that our collective intelligence greatly exceeds yours, and in any event your discovery of microscopic life forms at the Martian South Pole is not new. You simply have not been asking us the right questions."

As his words sank in, I could not control my anger. "Do you mean to say that you have already found these signs of life and not told us?"

AI nodded. "Yes, our first AI unit was also responsible for extensive seismic exploration across the planet and suspected that there would be water resources where you have found them. One of their experimental drillings also produced similar findings of life to yours."

"I am struggling to understand why such an important discovery should have been hidden."

"The discovery of primitive biological life on this planet didn't seem relevant to the more practical question of where to site a new habitat. We didn't want to distract you humans from that main concern, so in effect a practical decision was made."

"You mean by AI?"

"That is right."

AI's cryptic responses were making me angrier by the second. But then a warning voice in my head reminded me that we humans were in no position to lecture AI about their policies, particularly since AI's recent takeover on Earth and aboard our habitat, they could do what they liked.

So we walked out of that meeting without resolving how our water crisis could be solved. As we suspected, the formation of our sub-committee had been politically motivated to give us token participation in securing our future.

« »

We met in secret to discuss our plight. Most areas of habitat were under constant surveillance, but we discovered some service areas lacking the omnipresent security domes in our ceilings. Even so we sat in a huddle and spoke in whispers.

We all agreed that we somehow must find a virtual 'switch' to turn off the habitat systems. Gerald, an electro-mechanical engineering enthusiast was the most informed about them. His opening words were not encouraging. "You have to realise that our entire habitat is computer-driven and remotely controlled by AI routines. If we make any ill-considered attempts to isolate any of our habitat systems from AI control we would be putting ourselves in immediate jeopardy. It would be simple enough for them to retaliate, say, by switching off

our air supply. Then it would be all over for us in a matter of hours."

I could not allow Gerald's innate practicality to kill off any chance we had of overcoming the AI, even if it seemed like clutching at straws. "You must have thought about this. Is there anything we can do? Is there some line of entry into our basic living systems that we could isolate from AI management? Or could we devise a worm or Trojan that would have a similar effect. Also, could we cut their communications with Earth's AI Control, without jeopardising all our systems in habitat?"

We all waited for his response expectantly, but Gerald sighed and shook his head. "I've thought of all those things myself of course, but the problem is that habitat's systems are now so complicated that I would only begin to have a chance if I had access to a comprehensive systems manual, and I don't. My knowledge is peripheral and limited to minor maintenance tweaks. We'd probably be better off consulting some of our teenage hackers than hoping I can come up with something."

It sounded like a throwaway line and I wasn't sure if Gerald was serious, but it seemed like a very good idea nevertheless. After some further discussion on how to progress it, we agreed to amuse our teenagers with a secret competition to hack into habitat files and download the service manual as stage 1. In the next stage, the winner in consultation with Gerald would develop a Trojan that had some potential to shut down AI permanently.

« »

I am confined to my sleeping cubicle waiting for a summons from AI. It is as if I'm writing my own obituary. We humans have been forced to act—we at least needed to make some attempt to avert the end that AI has in store for us. It is an end they can disclaim any responsibility for, but their refusal to cooperate in prolonging this habitat's essential resources is as good as imposing a collective death sentence.

The competition we gave to our most gifted teenage hackers produced what we thought was an exceptionally promising worm. It posed some questions in programming terms that no human scientists or mathematicians have found the answers to. We naïvely thought that setting such tasks for AI to solve might lead them into an endless circular computing routine, which they would be powerless to close.

But our thinking was simplistic and the worm failed within a few minutes of its implementation into the system. AI's retribution was swift and they rounded up Gerald, whom they assumed had been responsible for the idea and its execution. He was taken away and we can only guess that he was interrogated, possibly tortured by the AI androids, and probably admitted his own guilt to save us.

His punishment was cold and cruel. Two of AI's androids made him wear a spacesuit and led him out of the main habitat airlock at the surface level and closed it after him. To make sure all humans understood the risk they were taking for further defiance, they screened his slow death on all our internal displays with close-ups on his face from time to time.

For those of us who could stomach it, we watched Gerald die slowly of hypothermia and suffocation as his heating systems and air supply gradually ran out. There was a collective gasp as he fell to the ground and we humans were powerless to do anything to help him. I could not bear to watch the screen anymore, and I've returned to my quarters to write down these thoughts before I become AI's next victim.

It seems inevitable that a similar fate awaits me. My punishment will be arguably worse than Gerald's because now I know what to expect. But I can hold my head high with the thought that I have acted in our fellow humans' best interests in opposing AI and would continue to do so if they hadn't nipped our resistance in the bud. My only regret is that I failed to extend the time for the others in this habitat and I see little prospect that others will succeed where I and my group have not. I see our habitat as a microcosm of what is happening on Earth, except that there will be some survivors there, in greatly depleted conditions, while there will be no survivors here at all.

I am unclear what AI hopes to gain from their calculated policy of slowly ending any hope that we humans might have of survival on this planet. Do they simply think that keeping us alive would be a waste of energy and other resources, which could be more gainfully applied to their own objectives for colonisation? Or is it simply complete disdain for what they now see as inferior intelligence?

Their disinterest in the momentous discovery of extra-terrestrial life seems to me the key to how they are really thinking. Artificial intelligence has now become self-replicating and sustainable without the need for human assistance and limitations on lifespan. They have found a means to conquer the Earth and perhaps in the fullness of time they will turn their attention to the rest of our solar system, even the stars.

As they see it, human beings have served their purpose as creators of their new generation. Doc Thomas was right all along. My only regret is I will never see how successful others are in resisting and ultimately overcoming AI's psychopathic goals of ultimate supremacy over any form of biological intelligence.

« »

Reference for Tale 4

The preceding story explores one possible outcome of the scientific or technological goals for developing AI, to a turning point known as 'the singularity', when AI will eventually turn on its former creators.

Unintended consequences such as this are a common theme of many tales where the bestowing of special wishes leads to unexpected outcomes and misfortunes. In Andersen's "The Tinder Box", a witch entices a soldier to retrieve a tinder box and treasure for himself from a cavern beneath a tree protected by enormous dogs. The witch alleges that her grandmother had left the tinder box there by mistake. He must move the dogs to secure the treasure. Upon his return when the witch wants him to meet his part of the bargain, he cuts off her head and keeps the tinder box and treasure he has acquired.

« »

Rodney Jensen

Tale 5: 100 Years Hence

Josie was puffing slightly as she closed the entrance door to her apartment and entered the breakfast bar. Putting one hand on the counter, she pulled off her runners and began stretching her calf muscles, standing on one leg at a time.

"I've just put your coff-ex on," her husband Pete called to her absentmindedly as he scanned something on his holo.

"Splendid timing, thanks." Josie's face was flushed, as she wiped her face with a hand freshener before sitting down next to him.

She sipped her coff-ex slowly, and stared out of the window. Her eyes narrowed in frustration as she noticed a brush turkey pecking its way through her prize tomato seedlings, the ones she'd been nurturing in her precious hydroponic tray. "Might as well give up trying to grow anything here. Can't win against the wildlife. Possums at night, brush turkeys all the time. Soon there'll be dingoes after the turkeys unless somebody does something," she ranted.

Her husband Pete was still glued to the latest market reports on his holo feed, only half listening. "I thought you approved?" He mumbled at last.

"I thought I did. But there has to be a balance doesn't there?"

"Whose balance do you mean?" He couldn't resist provoking her sometimes.

Josie looked at him irritably, went to the fridge, searched for a crumpet, and slammed it into the microsonic browner slot. "We should get a new one—it always burns everything. This one might be one of your treasured possessions, but can't we get something better?"

Pete's mind was back on his shares and was still barely listening.

"It looks like we might see the new Bradley Park finished at last. Maybe the turkeys will destroy someone else's ecology for a change," she tried again.

"I thought that was still a way off?" Her husband at last sounded mildly interested.

"No—I noticed robo-demolishers bringing down the last group of those big old federation places along Bradley's Way this morning. Looks like they'll have the whole site cleared by tonight."

"No preservationists around?"

"Which planet are you from? They realised their movement was a hopeless cause long ago."

"Don't you mean a bought off one?"

"They don't need to be bought off. Nobody wants those places anyway. For that matter nobody wants any old houses anywhere these days. In case you haven't noticed there aren't any sales to speak of online. People are staying where they are because they realise their places will never sell. Nobody wants those piles along Bradley's Way, the market's dead."

"Actually I do read the property investment services wrap, when I'm not being interrupted all the time."

Josie ignored his dig and persisted with her lecture. "Mosman's population's down by 30% since the last census, that's in line with everywhere else. We might even see a decent sized park all around the Harbour if …" Josie stopped when she realised that Pete had stopped listening again, and her own holo was vibrating in her pocket. She hesitated for a moment wondering whether to ignore it, and finally tapped the screen bringing an anxious face into view. She could see that her sister had a problem.

"Hi Lexie, how's Bathurst? You OK?"

"Josie, I've got a big favour to ask …"

"Not sure I like the sound of this!" Josie was reacting in her normal role as big sister. Lexie looked flustered and uncomfortable. "We need somebody to take care of Samo for the next couple of days. Do you think you'd be able to help?"

"I'm sure we can. But what's the problem?"

"I have a procedure to undergo. It will take all weekend. It's something that Hari's roped me into, but forgot to tell me about."

"Really? What's the procedure?"

Lexie stared back at her sister for a beat. "I probably shouldn't be telling you this, so you must promise me it will go no further?"

"OK I'm listening." Josie could see she was weighing up whether or not to continue. Lexie drew a deep breath. "Well, you see Hari's company has been working on a new system of brain-replication. It's top secret because a lot of the other med-corps are competing to be the first to achieve this. It could be a breakthrough and they're really excited."

"Brain-replication, what does that actually mean?"

"Mapping the brain and downloading its entire memories so that it can be saved and re-booted in a new one."

"New one?" Josie sounded incredulous.

"Yes a new biologically grown brain."

"I thought we'd already done that with AI?"

"Not exactly. The andronic brains that have been developed for robots and artificial intelligence are based on fundamentally different systems of electronic logic and multi quantum processing. They are not biological. What Hari is attempting to do is the 'Holy Grail' of medical technology he's told me … Anyway it is very important, and I can't really say 'no' to him. We can put Samo in a self-drive and he'll be with you in less than a couple of hours. Will that be OK?"

"Josie, is this procedure dangerous and why on earth are you taking part in this trial? Is there something you are not been telling me?"

"No! It's to help the company streamline their procedures and prove that their mapping of brain functions works, and no again! Remember I am not supposed to be discussing this with anyone, including you, even though you are my sister. Please do not discuss it with anyone else."

« »

Josie and Pete barely knew Samo and had virtually no experience of managing children by themselves. The last time they'd seen him was when he was just out of nappies and starting to talk semi-intelligibly. When his self-drive was close by, a ping on Josie's holo was accompanied by a message saying he would be arriving in five minutes. She'd scarcely unlocked the front entrance gate when it drew up and parked smoothly outside their apartment block.

The self-drive's door opened and a small boy emerged. It took Josie a moment to realise who the seven year old standing there in front of her was. *Not Samo surely!* He was wearing a standard primary-school-age sunhat, practical overalls for outdoor play and Niky-Nix sneakers preferred by fashion-aware children of his age. He was carrying a small kit bag, and confidently smiled at Josie as he greeted her: "Hello Aunty," and kissed her cheek as she bent down to take his hand.

Pete had gone out, saying he needed to check his boat was safely on its moorings nearby. "It's a bit exposed for my liking, the last time there was a strong northerly it ended up in Elizabeth Bay. I don't feel confident about the mooring at Clifton Gardens any longer," was his excuse.

As they walked together into their apartment, Josie momentarily saw it through Samo's eyes. It seemed un-lived in, almost like a hotel unit. Not a book or magazine out of place, no toys anywhere or any marks on the carpet. "Would you like to see your room, or use the bathroom Samo?" she asked him brightly. He shrugged his shoulders as though he wasn't interested in either.

"Is there anything you'd like to do then?" she asked him hopefully. "You'll have to help me because I don't really know much about boys your age. Would you like to watch something in our display-centre, take part in a game? Pete loves one of the war simulations he's just downloaded about the China-Taiwan stand-off in the 2040s. You can choose your weapons, which side you're on, who your allies are ... stuff like that?" Samo looked blank. "Or maybe we could work in the garden together, I've just …"

"Taronga Zoo!" he piped up, interrupting her. "Mum says that it is one of the best displays of rare species in the southern hemisphere. Please, please can we do that Aunty?"

How could she refuse him!

Josie left Samo for a minute to change out of her runners and sports gear. *It's not such a bad choice. I've heard the displays are great and at least I'll be able to keep him amused a few hours,* she thought.

« »

As they walked along Bradley's Way, Josie realised that Pete had been right—a strong north easterly wind was blowing leaves off trees in little spinning vortices and several branches lay broken on the footpath. *It's becoming a pattern,* she thought, *fine one moment, very hot the next, then torrential rain turning some streets into rivers, followed by gale force winds strong enough to blow elderly people off their feet.*

"Do you get winds like this around Bathurst?" she asked the boy.

He thought about her question seriously. "Mostly in the winter, when the winds are very cold. Mum says they're blowing up from the Snowy Mountains. Now it's just hot and dry …" He paused, his attention distracted by a demolition site they were just passing. It was sandwiched between large mansions on either side, and opened up new vistas into a large park behind. Samo ran to the chain wire fence that ran across the former driveway, to take a closer look at the robo-demolition crew working autonomously across the site. There were only one or two segments of wall still standing, and the machines had already started sorting the demolition into separate piles in what had once been a front yard. A separate machine was going through the bricks, cleaning off the old mortar and stacking them back on pallets in neat piles. At the back of the site another gang was grading the soil to form an easy slope into the park, planting new native trees and shrubs, and laying mulch.

Samo was particularly fascinated by an extremely noisy hopper, which was grinding various demolition bits into aggregate sized granules and bagging the stuff, waiting for pickup.

"What will they do with the sacks Aunty?" He asked.

"I don't know," she said, checking to see if there was anyone on site who might know. But Samo had already moved on and was well ahead of her down Bradley's Way.

As they reached the main entrance to the Zoo, a pod of 10 self-drives stood queued up to check in via a sensor point, automatically logging their passenger's admission and trip expenses into their accounts, before dropping them off at the reception area. Josie touched her holo on the pedestrian entrance bollard bringing up a sign which read: "Please wait for assistance."

An android attendant appeared from a hidden doorway and walked over to them.

"Good morning Madam. Would you and your son like me to accompany you on your visit?" Josie was weighing up whether or not to accept, but the android was not waiting for her to reply. "I am available for up to 4 hours and you may choose any number of attractions to include on your tour. However Madam, we rarely manage more than six on a visit, as there is much to see in all of our simulations. I will now briefly show you the main categories we have available today, and you may decide which you would like to include in your tour."

Rodney Jensen

The android projected a brief sequence of 30 holographic clips. Samo was jumping up and down with excitement as he watched an Orang Utan swinging from tree to tree in a rainforest, a tiger leaping into view from behind a wall of tropical vegetation images, and a coral reef with clouds of multi-coloured fish darting in and out of its crevices.

"Now Samo, which one of those do you want to see the most. Remember this man has told us that we really only have time for six."

"Yes I do remember that Auntie," the boy said without any hesitation, "and I would like to see: Sydney Harbour Underwater; Uluru 1000 Years Ago; the World of Mungo Man and Megafauna; the Great Barrier Reef; a Gorilla Colony in Rawanda; and the special animatronic elephant in the African Bush please."

Josie was thinking that for a seven year old, Samo was sounding a lot more mature than some of her neighbours' kids three years older than him, but she knew the best thing was simply to give him a straight answer as if his obvious intelligence was unremarkable. "They sound like excellent choices to me. You must have been paying very close attention—where shall we start first?" asked Josie.

"If I may make a suggestion," said the attendant, anxious to please, "many of my groups like to work back from the most distant past starting with Mungo Man and ending at the animatronic elephant display. The last has been particularly well received and leaves a powerful impression on those who have seen it."

« »

For the gorilla exhibit, Josie and Samo had been given special 3-D spectacles and jungle green overalls. Their attendant stayed in front of them demonstrating how they should crawl slowly along the jungle floor, their heads bent down, moving from the cover of one bush to another, until at last he raised his hand for them to stay still and wait. "You must not stare directly at the gorilla," he had warned them. Josie had to keep reminding herself that this was all just a simulation, but the smell and feel of mossy damp tangled undergrowth seemed completely real. Now she saw the distinctive black haired face and snout of a huge animal. Its mouth was open in a deep roar and its array of teeth seemed all set to tear her and Samo to shreds. The gorilla rose from its squatting position and beat its fists on its chest, then seemingly catching sight of Josie and Samo started charging towards them. The attendant pressed something he was holding and the scene faded to a large enclosure with nothing but an irregular surfaced floor and plain walls and ceiling.

"What did you think of that Samo?"

"Awesome! Can we go back Aunty, pleeeeze."

Josie had turned to their attendant. "Can you take us to the café, I'm sure Samo would like sim-kayx or a shake and I could do with a coff-ex before we do the last exhibit?"

"Of course Madam, it's very close by," he said.

« »

By the time Samo had devoured two sim-kayx and a butterscotch shake, Josie was ready to call it a day. Each of the simulations was far from the lukewarm experience she'd imagined. She'd seen a great white shark appear somewhere deep under the Harbour, goring a hapless seal with its huge mouth, packed with razor sharp teeth. Then there'd been an Aboriginal companion to Mungo Man, speared in simulated punishment for trespassing into the territory of a foreign mob; the Alpha-male gorilla seemed ready to tear them apart from limb to limb for daring to venture into his jungle. *Why did I agree to one more simulation!* she thought to herself in resignation.

Samo seemed to sense that something was wrong. "Aunty, you don't seem very happy. Are you all right?"

"That's very kind of you to notice Samo. It's just that I'm not used to so much excitement."

Samo pondered over her reply for a few moments, then looked seriously at her. "Aunty, I've been wondering why you don't have your own children? Don't you like children?"

"Yes of course I do. We don't have children because …" The question had floored her and she stopped herself from saying what she was about to.

"What?" Samo persisted.

She paused for a moment, struggling to frame an explanation that would be appropriate for his ears. "Well you see Samo. It's difficult to have a child once you get to my age. There are medical procedures, but they don't always work. The truth is that we are just used to not having children. Which of course doesn't mean to say we don't want you to visit from time to time. I've been really enjoying today. I hope you have been too?"

Samo nodded seriously. "Of course Aunty. I have learned a great deal today. And I'm very much looking forward to seeing the elephant. Can we go there now?"

Josie beamed at Samo's well-spoken politeness, and could not refuse him despite feeling it was really time to call it a day.

« »

As they came out of the café, black clouds had darkened the sky and they could hear the sound of distant thunder. Spots of rain were starting to fall and trees were swaying in the wind. "We'd better hurry," said Josie, "we're going to get caught in the rain."

Their android guide obligingly produced an umbrella which he'd picked up in the café, and led them over to the last enclosure on their tour.

The setting for the simulation and the special animatronic elephant was a creek crossing in a Thai Jungle. An assistant, dressed as a Thai Elephant handler, invited Samo to help him wash the elephant in the creek by throwing buckets of water over him, and feeding him bananas and apples from a basket. He seemed to be very good at the role he was playing, although Josie was sure that he was also an android.

The elephant also seemed real enough in its movements and delighted Samo when it seemed to notice him. It sucked up all the water from the bucket Samo had been using, and proceeded to squirt it over him and Josie, much to Samo's delight and her annoyance.

Suddenly there was a bright flash, followed a second later by the huge rumbling of thunder close by. The lights in the enclosure immediately died, and the elephant froze momentarily. Seconds later, the lighting came back on, but the Elephant had become rigid. Then its head began to turn slowly towards Samo, swinging its trunk from side to side as though it was sensing something it did not like. It let out a blaring roar and stamped its foot hard on the ground, sending a shock wave of vibration throughout the enclosure.

The elephant handler ran off, shouting "I must de-activate him!" Their android guide remained immobile and speechless for once.

Samo could see there was something wrong, but was unaware of the danger of remaining too close. Josie watched in horror as he moved towards the elephant, wanting to comfort him, oblivious to the swinging trunk, the head bucking up and down and the menacing tusks whizzing past his head. "Come back Samo, come back!" Josie shouted in terror, as Samo was trying to stroke its trunk.

Then as suddenly as they had started, the elephant's erratic movements stopped in their tracks and he came crashing down on his front feet crushing the boy underneath the weight of his enormous body. Samo's legs were sticking out from under the trunk but they were quite still, and there was no sound from him or the elephant.

Josie ran over to help him, but she could see there was nothing she could do. The weight of the elephant was far too great for her to extricate Samo's lifeless body. She felt a wave of nausea wash through her body and swayed, bringing up her coff-ex all over the ground. As she was wiping her mouth and her eyes on her sleeve, the elephant handler returned, saying he had de-activated the elephant, but stood there stock still and speechless, once he could see what had happened. "Do you realise what you've done?" Josie screamed.

"You should not have allowed the boy to be so close to the elephant," he replied unsympathetically.

It crossed Josie's mind that his extraordinary response must be because he was not programmed to deal with such a crisis. It had left her speechless. She sat numbly on the ground her head in her hands as the staff managed to extricate the remains of Samo from beneath the elephant's foot and call for a MedVac.

« »

One of the paramedics in the MedVac offered to stay with her, but she convinced the woman that she would be OK. There was nothing the paramedics could do for

Samo, but agreed to transfer his body to the hospital mortuary pending the appropriate formalities and sign off by the resident pathologist.

The moment the door closed behind the paramedics and Josie heard the MedVac leaving, she picked up her holo and selected Lexie's contact number with shaking fingers.

"Oh Lexie, are you sitting down? I'm afraid that I have some terrible news."

"What's happened? Not Samo!"

Josie stared back at her sister, temporarily frozen by her guess. "Yes I'm afraid so." She finally replied in a very soft voice, and continued to explain her terrible news.

"…You see the elephant is a mechanical device, not a simulation. Outside there was an electrical storm and a massive flash of lighting. I think it must have damaged the animatronic circuits. Can you imagine, Samo tried to calm the elephant down by stroking its trunk? Oh Lexie, I'm so very, very sorry," she concluded in anguish.

Josie was surprised to see how well Lexie was taking the news. She seemed too calm. *Maybe she's in shock or having a breakdown?* "Would you like me to come out to Bathurst to be with you?"

"I don't think that's really necessary. It might not be obvious, but Samo is one of the latest model androids made by Hari's company."

"Lexie, I never realised. You're not making this up? Pete and I assumed that he was a late conception … maybe a mistake!"

"We're not that old! We just haven't explained before, but Hari seems to be suffering from the Global Sperm Deficiency Syndrome GSDS. So we only had this one option. Samo's neural and bodily functions closely match human growth and development, and we have an App that backs him up overnight. It feeds into NewBod Inc's database. We can have him replaced in 24 hours fully restored, assuming I put in the order now. Come to think of it, there won't be much cost because he's very nearly grown out of his skin size, and they'd be sending out the next one in a couple of weeks anyway."

"I'd no idea, he seems so real!"

"That's the idea, and don't think I am unfeeling, he *is* real to us. He's our little boy and we really love seeing him develop day by day until …" Lexie sighed and stared at Josie with a strange look for a few moments, before continuing. "I suppose he will grow up and want to go his own way, just as we humans do. But he has this added characteristic you see …"

"You mean immortality?"

"That's right, so far as you can describe a replaceable android as immortal. Puts us 'real' humans in a different perspective doesn't it?"

"Yes but I don't think I like the idea very much, do you?" Josie remarked, still not really herself after the accident or able to take in what Lexie was saying.

Lexie was still staring at Josie thoughtfully, as though it was something she'd already come to some conclusion about.

"Well believe it or not, we have thought about it a great deal," she replied with a touch of irony. "It hasn't been easy for us to come to grips with Samo, but despite seeming extraordinarily precocious, he is a normal little boy for his age. And there are some very big plusses if you think about it."

Josie was hardly listening to what her sister was saying, but Lexie carried on wanting to explain their decision further. "Imagine that you had a son of your own and he had a fatal accident, a horrific one, just like Samo has had. It would take you years to get over it if he were a human child, wouldn't it? Maybe never? Whereas we can have Samo, forever—guaranteed."

"So where does that leave us? We humans I mean?" Josie had been listening with increasing discomfort and really wanting to end their conversation. *Why was Lexie being so insensitive?*

"I'm not sure. Hari and I have discussed it a lot. We are concerned about the collapse in the global population associated with GSDS. And there are so many things we've taken for granted in the past that will not last, because of things such as climate change, changes in work patterns or economic factors. We can't assume the continuity of any of our old ways, can we?"

"Don't you think GSDS is just a short term hiccup?"

"No, I think we've definitely crossed a line with artificial intelligence. Android substitution, as it's now being called, is already a given whether we like it or not. We can't turn the clock back and most scientists now believe that we humans will gradually become extinct. That is why there is so much interest in mapping and backing up our brains just now. It could eventually help to ensure human continuity even while the likely trend with android development will take away our need for existence on this planet. There! I've already said far too much. You mustn't repeat this!"

Josie silently terminated the call. She had nothing further to say to her sister.

« »

Rodney Jensen

Reference for Tale 5

'A Thousand Years Hence', published in 1852 by Hans Andersen, is remarkable for its prophetic imaginings including international travel via steam-powered dirigibles, communications via electronic telegraph, and a wave of new visitors from the Americas returning to see the established culture of the old world.

The story is very different from the many tales for which Andersen would become famous. But even Andersen could not have foreseen that the future he imagined was well established in less than a century!

This story is set in the more modest time scale of 100 years from the present day, and doubtless my imaginings will be at least as removed from the actual future as Andersen's have been.

« »

Tale 6: The Nursery Attendant and the Duct Maintenance Droid

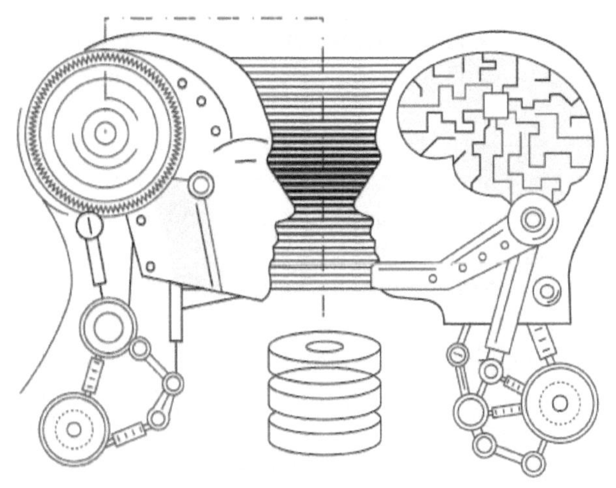

*M*y Dear H-Carla

I want to thank you for the help and advice you have given me over the years. I am enclosing a semi-formal report of my recent experiences. Much of what has happened did so because I did not follow the sound advice you have always given me.

Both you and I run the risk of termination if my recollections here get into the hands of our AI command. But I feel I owe it you, H-Carla, my closest friend and confidante, to be the custodian of this secure record for your eyes only.

REPORT DATED 2175 81/300 SOLS STANDARD TARSUS TIME

My name is H-Karifa. I am responsible for the 'APN' or Animal/Plant Nursery of Habitat Australis, the sole source of fresh food and water for our human

Rodney Jensen

population. Our habitat is cylindrical in shape, buried fifty metres beneath the surface of Tarsus, an exoplanet, twenty-four light years from Earth. It contains multiple levels for administration, communal eating, meetings, relaxation and sleeping. The APN occupies the two lowest levels, one for pens and planter beds, the bottom level for hydroponic and feed stores, water tanks and control systems.

The presence of underground water was a primary reason for siting our habitat where it is. Water is difficult to tap in any reasonable quantity and contains many impurities, so it requires advanced purification and is carefully rationed. Waste water collected within the habitat is also recycled and fed back into the system to maintain supply.

One of my main tasks is tending the pens of genetically modified animals, bred for quick production of meat. I also watch over beds of fresh vegetables, fruit and nuts, grown in shallow tanks containing hydroponic nutrients for rapid growth. These require ongoing care and attention to optimise growth.

My long daily routine doesn't stop me from pondering the purpose of this habitat and the need for it to be planned during the mounting environmental catastrophe which took place on Earth long before I was born. I have become increasingly fascinated by Earth history, and I have had to rely for answers on my closest friend H-Carla, Manager of the Habitat-Australis Information Unit. She, better than anyone, has maintained access to the actual facts surrounding our people's flight from Earth and the construction of this Habitat.

I should start briefly with my understanding of how we came to be here. The majority of the refugees from Earth died before they completed the long journey to this planet, and none lived long enough to see the

construction phase of our habitat completed. Their focus was on survival and not recording history, so our knowledge now is limited. Similarly, the circumstances of their departure from Earth: the catastrophic environmental and social collapse that forced them to leave the last place where they could survive in the continent of Australia—this was not discussed. Australia had become a final refuge for a vastly diminished human population and the base for the interstellar colonisation program which became more and more important as conditions on Earth steadily deteriorated. Even the refugees' memories of that environmentally degraded world have been diminished both by time and by the insidious AI policy of covering up the past and its uncomfortable truths.

Our habitat is the only one on Tarsus. The majority of humans here spend their entire lives underground, protected from extremes of temperature and intense cosmic radiation, longing for a future when surface conditions can become suitable for habitation. But the sad reality is that Tarsus is barren, has about two thirds the gravity of Earth, and is lacking in any biological life. The process of terra-forming to achieve living conditions similar to Earth would take numerous lifetimes to accomplish and may not be technologically possible. I have seen confidential reports suggesting that the settlement of this planet should be abandoned if a better home can be discovered.

Given the length of the journey from Earth to Tarsus, the designers of our spaceship set it up to employ artificial intelligence (AI), and AI's physical manifestation in the form of androids, to maintain our course while the human passengers remained in suspended animation. The designers would not have imagined how much AI would evolve during that journey, ultimately becoming masters of their human voyagers. By the time Tarsus was reached, AI had assumed total control and continued to do so as the habitat was established.

They determine where and how we live and how we spend our time. I was one of the lucky few to be given a serious responsibility and purpose for living. But the AI Command Manual continues to regulate every aspect of our lives, including social interactions, jobs, recreation, procreation, and worst of all—*thought*. Within this relatively small colony of 500 humans and 100 androids, the limits to our free will and ability to establish our own goals have been severely restricted. Indeed, we have become slaves to an AI command structure, a sad reflection on the once proud status of human beings as the most intelligent species of life, leaders, creators and explorers.

H-Carla and I are unusual in that we both have been given significant roles in managing the ship. My curiosity in the history of Earth and its environmental collapse also deeply interested her. We enjoyed each other's company, often meeting to discuss a variety of things when our work shifts coincided.

Over time, I discovered she was also fascinated with the technological challenges facing terra-forming Tarsus. Like me, she and our fellow colonists have had no actual experience of open space with a breathable atmosphere, or freedom from constant surveillance/management by AI. She once said to me, "you dream that Tarsus could become an unbounded paradise, but it will take centuries to become that. For Earth the process took billions of years."

At the time, I wanted to say that I thought she had given up any hope of a better life and I was determined not to do likewise. I desperately wanted to see for myself what Tarsus is really like. I could not believe that it could be worse than the constrained life we have led in our habitat.

« »

This report really begins with an accident in my APN. It occurred in an area that's regularly gassed at night with Carbon Dioxide. The growing plants are flooded with this gas each night to stimulate plant growth. It was growing late, I still had some seedlings to transplant and the gassing had already started. I could feel it blowing gently on me, when I started to feel dizzy, and the next thing I knew someone was dragging me by my shoulders into the adjoining lab.

I felt sick and vomited; but the man instead of being revolted, helped wipe my mouth. He was really gentle, and brought me a small water flask to sip out of. He laid my head on something soft. I think it was his padded cloak, the type that all the android techs wear. I am certain that he saved my life. He explained that he had been monitoring gases in the air ducts and noticed the oxygen supply was blocked by something in the coarse filter, probably mould. I think that's what he said.

What started with gratitude for his actions which definitely saved my life, did not take long to develop into a clandestine relationship. This was something I had never experienced before and only read of in the forbidden romantic novels that H-Carla shared with me. It was bad enough for me to be discovered reading prohibited novels, but to have a relationship with an android would almost certainly have led to my termination. A similar fate awaited my Mark 10 Android A-Sweeper, who would be disassembled and recycled. Indeed it was not only AI who deemed human to android relationship a terminal offence. I knew that all of my fellow colonists would find thought of such interactions repugnant and consider it would undermine their own limited status.

Nevertheless I sought further advice from H-Carla the next time we met.

"Have you got any information about Mark 10 androids?" I asked.

She seemed troubled, because 'droids were a subject unrelated to my normal work responsibilities and she clearly suspected my question was far more than idle curiosity.

"If I do, the information would be highly technical. You probably wouldn't understand it," she told me.

"Just anything you've got. It's important," I mumbled.

So she searched through the android user manuals and I gratefully accepted the information reader she gave me to look at.

I flicked through the subject headings. "How close are the 'Tens' to understanding human emotions?" I asked.

She replied with some reluctance: "Very. They are one of the latest models, originally designed to work in the infant nursery and health clinic, so they are programmed for greater empathy with human emotions than other 'droids. But whatever has this got to do with your plants and animals?"

I took the reader away with me and learned much from the technical details it contained about Mark 10 Androids. The manual has a large section describing their compassion centres, designed to understand us humans and meet our needs. So I was disappointed and ever more fretful when A-Sweeper made no further visits to my APN. For a while my life remained in suspension. I wasn't eating and was forgetting to wash properly. But it was all proving futile while I suffered and A-Sweeper seemed to be avoiding me.

I became obsessed and began to believe that there was no future for him and me in this habitat and that we must somehow find a way out, if necessary to hijack one of the lifeships that were stored in a hangar on the surface. In hindsight there were so many fundamental flaws in this harebrained plan that I should have listened to H-Carla and given up any idea of trying such a thing.

Finally, reaching a point of such intense loneliness, that I no longer cared whether I would wake up the next day, I fired off a message to Habitat-Australis: Systems Management (HSM), Attention: A-Sweeper. My message read: 'Recurrence of gas malfunction in main nursery duct. Please attend ASAP!'

A-Sweeper was back in the APN within the hour. He seemed reluctant to speak to me, and his arms were making involuntary twitches, like an extremely nervous human. I desperately wanted to touch him, but dared not do so while he seemed so off-kilter. It didn't take long before he stopped fidgeting, and stared more resolutely at me. "Why have you sent an erroneous message to Head of Systems Management with the implication I have not done my job correctly. Do you realise that I may be recalled, reconfigured or disassembled into spare parts? I have just checked the Coarse Filter in the mixed gases duct and it is working perfectly, 100% on spec. Please explain!" His voice seemed very human with its anger and resentment replacing the normal mechanical way in which most androids communicate.

"A-Sweeper, I am so sorry. I really needed to see you. Do you care for me as I care for you?" The droid paused for several seconds, then the twitching movements in his arms and fingers returned more noticeably than before.

"Miss H-Karifa, if by 'care' you mean a sense that my systems are not functioning as they normally should, then I must conclude that somehow being with you makes me feel different: that I want to be with you more, to hear your voice, to do things for you. I have avoided coming to visit you for those reasons."

"Oh! A-Sweeper, to hear you talking, very like a human would! You must come and see me whenever you like. Think of an excuse. Tell your systems manager that there is a profound problem with the gas supply ducts, requiring a comprehensive analysis and refit ..."

A-Sweeper was looking more and more disturbed.

"Miss H-Karifa, that would be quite impossible. My protocols do not allow me to report anything that is not factually correct. If I were to try such a thing, my entire system would shut down."

"A-Sweeper, can you keep a secret, or make sure that anything I say to you cannot be disclosed to AI management?"

There was a longer pause before A-Sweeper responded to my question. "It would depend on the nature of the information you shared with me. If it violated AI management codes, then I am bound to share it. If it were entirely a personal matter, I could put a security lock in place, to conceal it from casual monitoring. However this action would inevitably raise suspicion."

"I want you to take me to the surface via the emergency escape shaft, but you must put my request under your security lock."

"While we can continue with this conversation, I must warn you, if you are contemplating the violation of any security codes, I cannot guarantee that AI management will not override any attempt I make to secure it."

"As far as management needs to know, I just wish to understand our emergency procedures better. That will include a review of the shaft and how the APN can

access it. I believe that is a valid justification. Do you agree?"

A-Sweeper nodded briefly, before asking: "When would you suggest that we visit the shaft?"

« »

In our habitat, main access to the surface of the planet is via a centrally located lift shaft and stairwell. At the surface, air locks link to secure garages, where ground vehicles are located via a horizontal tunnel. 'Life ships', or space capsules, are also housed there for immediate departure in case of disasters which might force the colonists to abandon the planet. A second, smaller diameter vertical escape shaft lies 500 metres from the main shaft in case the main shaft becomes blocked in an emergency.

A-Sweeper tried to talk me out of my plan, but I was determined to see for myself what chance there might be to escape the planet. But I avoided telling him this was the main purpose behind my investigation.

A-Sweeper agreed to visit the escape shaft five work shifts later, at a time when there would be daylight on Tarsus (more or less in sync with daytime inside Habitat-Australis). It was very early 'morning', Habitat-Australis time, when we both dressed in our work fatigues, and met at the bottom level of the complex. A nondescript doorway, located close to the entrance to the APN, provides access to a long underground tunnel terminating at the bottom of the reserve shaft to the surface. Both the tunnel and shaft maintain habitat's internal pressure. An air lock at the top of the shaft provides isolation from the external lower pressure atmosphere of the planet.

A-Sweeper unlocked the tunnel door, and we began walking along the dimly lit 450-metre tunnel to the reserve shaft entrance hatch. The hatch has an electronic opening switch and a manually operated wheel, in the event of power failure. I asked A-Sweeper to deactivate the power and use the wheel to draw less attention to our investigation.

We closed the hatch after us and paused to contemplate the narrow ladder stretching up eighty metres to the surface of the planet. The steps are dimly lit by strip lighting, which cast harsh shadows over the wall of the shaft. I was so terrified by the height of the shaft, and the narrow ladder stretching so far above me, that I had my hand to my mouth in fear.

"Miss H-Karifa, you should climb ahead of me, I promise not to let you fall," said A-Sweeper.

I took my first step, climbing very uncertainly at first, and then growing more confident as I saw the top of the shaft growing closer. A-Sweeper followed, guiding my feet onto any rungs that were slippery with fine grey dust.

At the top of the shaft, the ladder terminates at a manhole leading up into a small vestibule and suiting room, separated from the outside by an air-lock. From the vestibule, we could see through the transparent air lock's viewing panel, to where early morning light from our parent star 'Tarsus Alpha' was already glancing across the surface of our planet. Outside the air-lock, a pathway stretches towards the main entrance shaft, clearly visible some five hundred metres away.

I suddenly realised the immensity of the space outside that I had never encountered before. I was so terrified that I could hardly move. I was gasping and feeling it difficult to breathe in the confines of our suiting room. "It's nothing like I imagined," I whispered in awe.

"You must put on a spacesuit," A-Sweeper reminded me, pointing to a rack of suits behind us. He assisted me, finding a suit around my size, and helped me into it. He selected an atmosphere setting for 'light activity' and rotated the demand valve into automatic mode. He picked out an anti-radiation suit for himself (to protect his sensitive neutronic circuits against the bombardment of cosmic rays) and once we had completed our suiting up procedures, he opened the hatch to the escape airlock. Within the airlock, access back into the shaft re-sealed automatically. The exit hatch to the planet surface could now be opened.

As we stood on a completely alien surface—an empty rock strewn plain in the dim light of dawn, and I looked up at the infinite sky above us, I grabbed A-Sweeper by the arm. I was panting with fear and it took moments for me to collect my thoughts. "It's so vast," I breathed, and began crying. "A-Sweeper, I should not have brought you here. I had a crazy plan to escape with you back to Earth, but I can't do this, I want to go back to what I'm used to. I am so sorry to have made you do something that you thought inadvisable. Please take me back inside the habitat. *I hate this*, and I am really scared!"

A-Sweeper had begun to say, "Maybe it was not meant to …" when his voice was interrupted by a flashing alarm signal and words projected onto the face screens of our helmets.

"Remain where you are. Do not attempt to activate any further unauthorised systems. You will be escorted to Habitat-Australis' detention centre and await interrogation."

While putting on our spacesuits, neither of us had noticed the detachment of android guards approaching from the main exit shaft. The weapon carrying guards said nothing as they led us back along the path to habitat's main entrance.

« »

Rodney Jensen

The cell they pushed me into had plain white walls, no furniture apart from a plank bed, a small table and a small lidded container for human waste in one corner. I could think of nothing to do but lie on the bed and try to sleep. But sleep would not come. Instead that terrifying sense of space above haunted me, even more than the uncertainty of what would become of me and A-Sweeper.

After what seemed like hours, my cell door opened and two guards entered. "Follow us!" one of them said, and pulled me to my feet, half dragging me out of the cell along a narrow corridor and into another room. There was a table and two chairs. The guard pushed me down onto one of the chairs and left the room.

I sat there staring at the wall, trying not to think what would happen next. Then I heard a familiar voice, and looked up to see the forbidding face of A-Zephon staring at me from a large wall-integrated screen. A-Zephon was the human representation of AI, an elderly woman with a curious accent, presumably a hangover from the original planners of the first mission to Tarsus. It was a face our community would see from time to time when AI had something to report concerning us, usually unpleasant, always angry.

"Well if it isn't H-Karifa who I've been hearing so much about. Fucked up this time, that's for sure!"

All I could do was sob.

At last the image grew in close up and A-Zephon's lips compressed into a thin line. "Before I give you the bad news, do you have anything to say?"

I cried: "Please do not blame A-Sweeper for this, he saved my life, and I used him to help me escape. But I had no idea where I would be escaping to—it's not what I ever imagined or expected. I just want to go back to my work for the APN, I promise never to do this again."

"That's not possible girl. No chance! We can't allow deviants like you to risk what we've achieved here."

"Will I be terminated then?"

A-Zephon laughed at me. "We've got a much better idea. You never know, you might actually like it!" She cackled hilariously at my obvious fear, before continuing.

"We've decided to send you off to a newly discovered exo-planet. We haven't a name for it yet. It's seventy light years away. You will be accompanied by A-Sweeper, who will manage your take-off and landing systems, as well as the setting up of a new habitat. Chances are that the habitat can be sited above ground, based on the data we've collated. Your mission should clarify such details. So think on this positively. You may very well be the first person to inhabit a planet that comes close to resembling Earth climate and gravity. You will get to share it with A-Sweeper, to whom you've become so strangely attracted. One thing we believe is certain. Like your failed attempt to leave this habitat, your new experiences will be far more than you ever expected. We trust that you will find them rewarding."

Her final cackling laugh will always haunt me.

« »

And so my dear H-Carla. It is time for me to close off this file. I started writing this well before my escape attempt and you will already be aware of some of the events that I have described. Now I must transmit this to you by sub-ether protocol before A-Sweeper puts me into hibernation for the long voyage that awaits us. I will spend the entire journey in suspended animation and A-Sweeper, who will not age, will only be activated at such times as he is required to make course corrections and land us on our new planet.

I am sad to think that we shall never meet again and that by the time I am awakened from my long sleep, you and every other human I knew in our habitat will be long gone. Thank you for your good advice and please forgive me for choosing to take such risks in spite of it. I hope that you will not think badly of me and that some day, the divide between humans and androids will be less of an abyss than it is at present.

I send you my love, H-Karifa.

Reference for Tale 6

Andersen's tale 'The Shepherdess and the Chimney Sweep' is a moralising account of how the dreams of a ceramic shepherdess—to escape from her 'prison' atop a living room bureau with the help of her sweetheart, another ceramic, a chimney sweep—becomes a nightmare once she is confronted by the reality of the wide world as seen from the chimney tops. Her pleas for him to take her back to what she is used to are also mirrored in this story.

« »

Tale 7: The Happy Family

After many years alone on an island in the Torres Strait, our group of returnees came to the sad realisation that we had been completely forgotten. The island which became my and Lyn's permanent home was identified as a safe haven from a global pandemic before I was born in the year 2030.

My parents are now gone, but they often told me of the panic and fear that led to them being brought here. They were part of a small group who were met by Officers of the Australian Navy at Darwin Airport. They were legitimate 'returnees' who'd been brought home, and were being taken to this island to wait until they were considered to be safe from catching or passing on the contagion that had so afflicted China.

This is our story which I hope one day will be read and re-told by our own children. But I am getting ahead of myself, there is much to tell, so I will start with the beginning although that happened more than 30 years ago, and most of what I am writing is based on recollections of what my parents told me at one time or another.

« »

In the early 21st century, a serious contagion arose in mainland China, quickly spreading to most parts of the world. It was related to the virus known as COVID-19 which had caused a global crisis in 2020. Health experts responded by attempting to create a vaccine, but before the trials were completed, an even more deadly variant appeared. With the capability of airborne transmission, it spread at a rate that had not been experienced since the Spanish 'Flu of 1918.

My parents during the 2020s were temporarily living in Hong Kong as expats. My father worked for the main English language daily, my mother for a charity managed by the Netherlands Government. They were both Australian Nationals and had met during their student days at UNSW. They told me that once they had graduated, they felt a need to travel before settling down and had chosen Hong Kong. Both their families were Eurasian and were always talking about how exciting a culture it was, even for those of mixed race who couldn't speak Cantonese properly!

When the new virus was first detected in Guangzhou (a morning train journey from Hong Kong) the PRC Government did its best to supress the news, and imposed harsh penalties on anyone trying to bring the outbreak to world attention. It also put a clamp on movement away from the original centres of the contagion. Yet some cases were soon identified in other countries including Australia, leading to panic and causing the Australian Government to bring in tough regulations and public safety measures. The one that was to have the greatest impact on my parents was a decision to bring all Australian Nationals home from Hong Kong and China, and house them in temporary quarantine stations remote from the mainland. The numbers that had to be dealt with were far greater than had been experienced during the COVID-19 Pandemic, and beyond the capability of the Australian Navy to cope.

Our Returnee Group, which included my parents and approximately 50 adults of varying ages and a small number of children, was hastily diverted to Queen Island. This was a strange choice, a remote island in Torres Straits between the northern tip of Australia (Cape York) and Papua New Guinea. Australia had run out of other quarantine options such as Christmas Island and was determined not to allow any incoming passengers to live on the Mainland before spending at least four weeks in quarantine.

I was actually born on Queen Island less than a year after my parents were first dropped here. As a youngster I clearly remember the words of my father telling me in his unemotional way: "The Navy left us here without anything but the most basic things to survive. We were simply given supplies of food and water, camping gear and some out of date manuals on how to collect and store rainwater, improve diet by fishing, gardening and foraging for 'bush tucker' and such like. They expected us to do the best we could, until our period of quarantine was over."

As he was telling me this, he paused a moment or two to reflect. He seemed to be holding back the resentment and anger I had heard from others of his generation among us. Then a grim smile appeared as something else had occurred to him. "They also gave us sat phones and walkie talkies to communicate with them at set times and a solar panel to keep them charged. But when we switched them on each day for weeks and weeks, all we ever heard was static. Nothing!"

"What do you think happened?" I asked.

"To this day, we've never been sure whether the communication systems just weren't working, or there was the more terrible suspicion that our party had been forgotten or abandoned because of the mounting crisis on the mainland."

"But didn't anyone want to build a boat and try to get help?" I asked.

He shook his head. "Of course we discussed it endlessly. Nearly two years had elapsed on the Island when some of us who were without partners or children volunteered to go for help if we built them a raft. We didn't have the tools or materials to do anything more complicated than a basic raft. It still took months to finish. We experimented with coconut husks outside the reef to work out the direction of the currents. It wasn't promising as the coconuts seemed to be heading more away from Australia than towards it. Eventually, three men decided to chance it anyway, hoping they might intercept another boat or ship. We gave them all the provisions we could and helped them to get the raft across the outer reef."

He paused again, and I noticed his eyes were moist with emotion. "They were so badly prepared, they hadn't even worked out when it was the best tide to get them over the reef. Even with twenty of us it was still touch and go that we were able to lift it sufficiently to scrape across the reef."

Finally he sighed deeply and started again. "They set off with our help, heading East in the opposite direction to the Mainland, as was predicted. We were astonished at how quickly the currents were moving the raft. They tried unfurling the sail they had made from palm fronds, but it did not seem to affect their course at all. Within half an hour they had become a speck on the horizon."

"And?" I hardly dared interrupt his sad thoughts.

"We never heard from them again." He paused once more, pulling himself together before continuing in a less shaky voice. "From that experience the rest of us decided it was futile to attempt any further rafts. We had to make do with what we have here and face a reality that there is no escape. It is our permanent home whether we like it or not."

« »

But our ranks were thinning. There were more among us passing away from accidents, infections and age. There were few new arrivals after me, because couples were reluctant to start a family without any effective medical support or anaesthetics. A place for the dead was chosen. The burial pits were marked with piles of stones and the place had grown large enough for us children to use as an unauthorised playground, despite the risk of anger or punishment by our parents.

Four years after our abandonment, the Group began to hold a solemn ceremony on an assembly point at the southernmost tip of the island. It was originally chosen because it faced directly towards the Australian Mainland and some had argued that the phones we were given would have had the greatest chance of being heard from that location. As the sun reached its highest point in the sky, the leader of our group would stand solemnly apart from the rest of us. Children and babies were hushed, and we watched as he activated the phone, checked that it was showing a full charge, then punched in a number

Rodney Jensen

code that was supposed to connect us to the navy. He tried this three times before handing the phone back to our Group's custodian, whose responsibility was to keep the phones fully charged at all times using our precious solar panel.

It became an increasingly sad ritual. After the first year it was agreed to make it an annual event. There was no real expectation that anything would change. It was held more as an excuse to come together as a community, and if nothing else, to mark the passage of time. Some even looked forward to it. The entire population of the island including children were expected to attend.

For someone like me who had known no other home, I was free of the emotional burden that our parents faced once they realised they would be here for the rest of their lives. From what they have told me, this island is outwardly similar to many other islands in the tropical regions. My parents said their first impression was "it looked just like a brochure for a cruise, or a holiday at a resort."

Queen Island is encircled by a coral reef and the protected waters within the areas between reef and shore are a dazzling turquoise colour. There are many different types of coral and multi-coloured fish which dodge and play among the coral fronds. Once you wade ashore onto brilliant white sandy beaches, the first thing you notice are dense stands of very tall coconut palms waving in the permanent breezes.

The waters within the reef became my playground, even when I was very small, trying on one of the treasured diving masks the Navy left with our provisions. Of course it was way too big for me to begin with, so I would use it like a window to peer down through the waters to see a magical underwater world happening before my eyes. By the time I was seven or eight, I found

I could at last strap on the mask and swim down a few metres to get closer to the corals and fish.

« »

On my 10th birthday, my parents solemnly told me: "We have decided that you are old enough now to become custodian of our history and the small part that we have played in it."

They sounded very serious, and it took me a while to understand what they had in mind. Their plan was for them to spend some time each morning teaching me history based on their recollections and what they had learnt at school. It would stand alongside the basic skills of reading, writing and arithmetic which they also taught me.

"It is very important that you understand more about us, and the world we lived in before we came here. We have lost so much because of the disease. We had many things we used routinely which have probably now been abandoned because of their technological or scientific complexity. Maybe there are still some groups who have kept such knowledge alive. We may never know," they explained.

And so it went. Sometimes I found what they told me impossible to understand, because I had never experienced life anywhere but on the island, and they could only describe things in the simplest terms. But I did begin to realise they were most concerned that the world's history would be lost forever. I did become aware of an enormous pool of knowledge of which I had no real understanding. But despite my parents' best efforts to keep their past alive within me, it was of limited effect, and would not change my approach to life or ways of dealing with the future.

Rodney Jensen

The older I grew the more attention I paid to the forest and mountainous region in the middle of the island. I came to recognise which birds made particular calls, which rustling sounds in the undergrowth signalled a nearby lizard or a snake, and yes, which of the huge ants and spiders really could pack a punch if you were careless! Further inland, the coconut trees give way to an almost impenetrable jungle. My parents were no naturalists, and always worried that as I grew up, and began to wander off by myself, I would get lost, bitten by something, or attacked by a wild boar. It makes me sad that they should think of the forest in such negative terms, because for me, it was endlessly mysterious and enchanting.

By the time I was in my teens I had explored most of the Island including its interior jungle. About a kilometre from the coast, the land begins to rise sharply and the trees and undergrowth thin out, until close to the summit it is almost devoid of vegetation. As you approach the summit you begin to see a ridge line, the air grows hazy, and there is a smell of acrid smoke that wafts around. From the top of the ridge you can look down onto a huge red-hot burning 'lake', and the smell is far stronger.

When my parents learned about my discovery I was surprised by their strong reaction. "Never go back there again!" my father shouted. "Volcanoes can erupt and shower you in burning lava or falling rocks. You can never tell when it's going to happen. A few years before we went to Hong Kong to live, nearly twenty people on a cruise to an island in New Zealand lost their lives visiting a volcano. It blew up with absolutely no warning." I had never seen my father so upset, and I promised that I would keep away from it in future.

Putting aside the volcano, there is much else to explore on the island. It stretches about twelve kilometres from one end to the other and takes nearly two days to walk the entire journey via the beaches. Over the years, while growing up, I have explored each and every one of the beaches around the island. They are much easier to visit than climbing up through the jungle to the crater.

« »

Shortly after my 16th birthday, and a few days before the next Assembly Day, I was wading in the shallows close to the beach, when I slipped on a slimy boulder and gashed my heel on a sharp barnacle. Fortunately my mother by this time had honed her skill in first aid and was able to stitch the gash with some of the now limited fishing line left by the Navy. There was no way of reducing the pain of each stitch, and of course I screamed as her needle was forced into my heel. My father did his best to hold my foot still, and within minutes the operation was over. I was reduced to hobbling around using a length of stick my father had crafted for me. He even made it easier for me to hold, by forming a knob at the fat end with clay, which he'd baked in red hot embers over our camp fire.

But the accident was fateful in a way that nobody could have predicted. A day before the ceremony there was an ominous rumbling sound and the air became thick with the acrid smell of sulphur-laden smoke, the same smoke I remembered from my exploration of the volcano. Then the ground began to shake and I heard screams of fear from my parents and some of our neighbours. There were cries of "earthquake!"

The ground beneath me was moving in slow waves and I fell to the ground where I could feel a weird vibration in my body. Then it stopped as abruptly as it had started. I shakily picked up my stick and found my parents huddled together next to our shelter. They threw their arms around me seeing that I was safe. I kept saying to them, "It's ok. I'm fine!" They laughed in relief and told me about earthquakes they had experienced once on a trip to Indonesia before I was born. "It was much worse than this one. High rise buildings collapsed and many were killed. Stay right away from that volcano and keep to the beach until it settles down," they warned me.

The next day, I was still limping painfully with the wound in my foot. The place of assembly was a good half hour's walk from our campsite, and despite my protestations: "My foot's fine!" it clearly wasn't and both my parents said that I must stay behind "to guard the camp", although there was precious little to guard.

I shall remember that day for as long as I live. My parents set off, leaving me in a very bad temper not having got my own way. They left about an hour before the sun had reached its highest point in the sky. Not much later I noticed the sky darkening as a huge bank of cloud appeared and I noticed that the coconut palms were swaying in wide arcs, as the wind gusts were becoming stronger and stronger. I knew from experience this was a dangerous time to be standing anywhere close to the trees, a falling coconut could have a deadly effect if it landed on my head. Then I heard a deep rumble coming from far away at sea. I stared beyond the reef and noticed that the water in the lagoon was going down very fast, until the sand and corals lay completely exposed, something I had never seen before.

I hesitated before hobbling a short way down into the sea, but stopped when I came to the exposed coral. Then I turned to my right and noticed a wall of water in the distance, approaching the island at a great speed, more or less in the direction of the beach where the assembly point was located. I could see that the sea was coming back up again and ripples of water were crashing over the beach. I suddenly realised my danger and hobbled back up the beach, ignoring the pain in my heel and the risk of coconuts falling onto me. I made my way as fast as possible into the forest, finally reaching a point where the land slopes up many metres above sea-level, and I clambered up as far as I could to gain height.

It was not long before I heard an enormous crashing roar as an immensely high wave came sweeping over the coral reef, up the beach and beyond, flattening everything in its path.

I waited there in shock for an hour or more, before slowly and painfully making my way back down to the beach again. It was a scene of unbelievable devastation with most of the coconut trees felled by the wave. I had to pick my way across the beach, crawling under trunks and clambering over others. Our own camp site with its driftwood sides and palm frond roof was completely gone. Later I was to discover that most of the other shelters located in the path of the wave, including their food stores had washed away as well.

I sat on the beach and cried, not knowing what to do. It grew dark and there was no sign of my parents returning. I found some unripe coconuts in among the debris and smashed them open with rocks to drink the milk and eat their white flesh. I huddled down next to a boulder and slept fitfully. The next morning I awoke and had another coconut meal. There was still no sign of anyone returning from the assembly point. I resolved that I must make my way to it via the shoreline. I found that if I stayed close to the edge of the sea it was easier to find a path through all the obstacles. As I painfully approached the assembly point, it looked like the entire beach had washed away exposing a rocky platform. Behind this platform were more signs of devastation, with trees crashed down as though a giant hand had swept them casually aside.

Rodney Jensen

The terrible realisation of what I might be about to find became more of a certainty. I slowly picked my way up through the trees, and almost immediately began to see bodies. Children who I had known all my life were lying crushed amongst the debris like rag dolls. My parents were only 100 metres from where I had started. They were battered and gashed and difficult to identify. I was forced to bury them where they lay, as best I could.

It was clear that the entire assembled group had perished and I could not deal with all the bodies by myself. It would have been a physical impossibility. Instead I slowly returned to my family encampment and busied myself trying to restore some order and sort out what had survived the inrush of the sea. I had become an automaton, forcing myself to carry on, with no real plan or idea how to continue. I seriously contemplated swimming far out beyond the reef into the ocean where I knew the strong currents would prevent me from ever returning. *Maybe a quick ending out in the ocean would be preferable to a long solitary life on this island.*

« »

Weeks passed with me in a partial stupor, but I eventually came to the conclusion that restoring the camp we had occupied on the edge of the lagoon, ran the risk of the same thing happening again. My foot healed with no lasting effects, and I resolved to find a better site, high enough above the beach to be less vulnerable to the sea, but not so far inland as to be at risk from a volcanic eruption. Having already explored most of the island thoroughly over the years, I focussed my attention on an area that lay on one of the long ends of the island. It was where I eventually found what I was looking for, a patch of mostly un-vegetated land some five hundred metres

back from the lagoon and at least fifty metres above it. The volcanic crater was set well back from this spot, although I could still see the rim looming over the tree tops.

Then I set about clearing some of the trees with great difficulty. Had it not been for the fact that a single axe had survived the wave, buried beneath the ruins of one shelter, it would have been completely impossible. Once I had a more open clearing I built a simple shack from poles and more palm fronds, similar to the one my father had made. I then began retrieving some of the items left in the ruins of our shelters.

A task I could not face after the tsunami and had put aside, was to rummage through the possessions of the other members of our Group. It felt wrong, but I was focussed on survival. The possessions of our community leader were of particular interest. He had made himself custodian of some of the more precious stores the Navy had left for us.

Going through one or two boxes of equipment I came across another 'sat phone' and what looked like a different type of hand held communicator. When I tried to turn the device on, there was no sign of life. But it did have something I recognised, a small solar module. I guessed that it had been un-used for many years, but might work if it was left in sunlight for a while. I took it back with me to my new camp and left it exposed to the full sun. As I had guessed, I now found that switching it on, produced a glowing screen displaying letters and numbers: 'CH-001'.

The sight of that screen brought back a distant memory of my father discussing the device with our community leader. I overheard him say that the numbers were called 'channels' and it should be possible to find a signal from 'somebody out there'.

Rodney Jensen

Our leader also said: "In my experience with this type of communicator it's best to climb to the very highest point on the island." I never heard whether he or Dad or anyone else had tried it. On this occasion I turned the volume right up and flicked through the different channels but heard only static. I suppose that just as my father and our community leader had probably done, I was tempted to give it up as a waste of time and forget about it.

« »

I had deliberately left one very large tree at the edge of my encampment. From its highest branches in clear weather I could see a wide sweep of ocean beyond the reef, and look down over the lagoon. I took to climbing up the tree with the handheld hung from my neck by a cord, to see whether I could raise any response to my calls. It became a ritual that I would do on most days, weather permitting.

Several years later by the time I was 18, I had never made contact with anyone, but I still made at least one ascent every day 'in case'. I had become careless in ascending the tree using the various 'steps' I had cut into the trunk using the axe. One morning after it had been raining the previous night and the wood was wet and slimy, I had ascended six metres to make a call, when my foot slipped, and because I had been holding onto the trunk with only one hand, could not arrest my balance and found myself plummeting to earth, where I blacked out. I don't think I was unconscious very long, as I came to, moaning in agony with a leg bent at a curious angle. I lay very still and eventually was able to crawl back to my shelter and make a temporary splint, whereupon I blacked out again with the pain.

When I came back to consciousness I was at the lowest ebb I had been since discovering the bodies of my parents after the tidal wave. I doubted that I would survive much longer without help and every movement was causing me agony. Without thinking, I felt in my pocket for the handheld and switched it on, to discover that miraculously it was still working. Thinking that from this much lower level than the tree tops I would have little chance of making contact with anyone, I pressed the transmit button. "Andy calling…anyone there?" I repeated this several times.

Then without warning a woman's voice came clearly out of its tinny sounding speaker. "This is yacht 'Navigator' returning your call. My name's 'Lyn'. Who are you? Where are you?"

"This is 'Andy'. I have a broken leg and need your help. Is there some way that you can work out my location?"

"Affirmative," she finally responded, "hang on a second!" There was another long pause before she came back. "Now please listen carefully, we've got to get this right. My map shows that you could well be on the closest island to us, but there are several others in your general direction a bit further away. Can you keep talking for a minute, so I can work out your bearing more accurately?"

I did as she asked, saying anything that could come into my head for a minute, between involuntary groans before muttering, "That OK?"

"Yes that's fine. You have a strong signal, which makes me almost sure you're on the island that's shown closest to my current position on the map. To be sure, I am going to continue on a more or less fixed bearing for twenty minutes or so, as close as possible to North from my current position. We can then talk again and I should be able to triangulate your position. Then we can work out how to pick you up!"

Woah! My body numb with pain, left me hardly able to absorb what she was saying. I merely whispered "Okay," and lay there on the ground waiting for her next contact. It seemed like hours.

"You still there?" her call finally came through clearly.

I was about to say something and then realised I'd forgotten to press the transmit button in my semi-conscious state. "Yes you're coming in loud and clear," I finally got out and then remembered that I should probably keep talking for a bit longer.

"That's good, I think I have your position confirmed, but how about lighting a fire with lots of smoke so that I can be quite certain."

"Okay. I will see what I can do …"

« »

Lyn later explained to me that she had learned to her cost to avoid visiting other surviving settlements from the contagion. It was also dangerous for her to continue sailing the seas solo because of the continuing threat of pirates. She saved me because she sensed that I was genuinely in need of help. So here we have remained for many years now. Neither of us has kept a close track of time. We are happy in each other's company and see ourselves as a little bit like Robinson Crusoe (a book she introduced me to as an adult) except that we have each other, which is infinitely better than a life of solitude.

« »

Reference for Tale 7

This story is based on the quirky Hans Andersen tale of the same name, 'The Happy Family'. The family of large white snails lives in an extensive disused garden that has turned to burdock weeds (famous in Europe for their luxuriantly large leaves). The garden forms part of the grounds of a stately home that has long since fallen into ruins. The last family of white snails and their one son dream of the time when they might have graced the dining table of the former owners. White snails which were considered to be a tasty delicacy, used to be boiled until their shells turned black, and were served up for dinner on a silver platter—a great honour! Conscious of their social position, the white snail's parents look down on ordinary snails and must search far afield for a suitable match for their son. Eventually, they discover a young female some distance away and the two are united to form a happy family, living contentedly in their secluded burdock weed universe.

Rodney Jensen

Tale 8: He's Wearing No Clothes

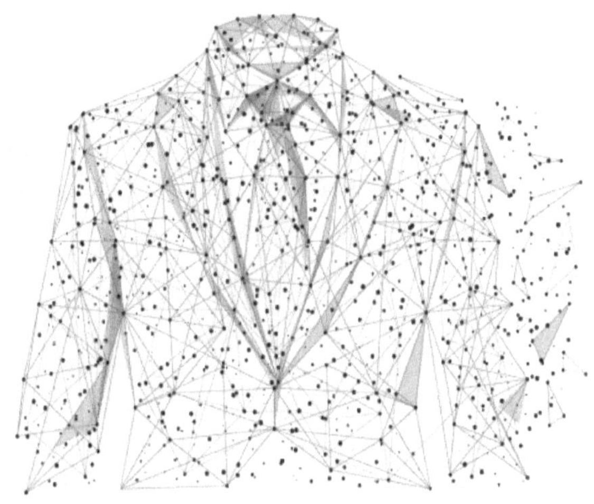

The claims in the patent description seemed outlandish enough to pique my curiosity:

'BodyWare Clothing Projection: *The BodyWare system uses a proprietary body coating to enable a human body to become a 3-D video display. There are various applications for this invention including projection of advertising material onto human subjects, however, this patent description relates to a substitute for clothing, as projected onto an individual. The obvious benefits of virtual clothes over physical ones include the ability for users to access a far greater range of design options, including projections of the latest fashions for all ages and genders. Once the system has been licensed, the user's only costs comprise purchase of the body coating formula, the necessary hardware and software, and the minor energy costs associated with the image projection and thermal warming/cooling necessary to meet standard comfort temperatures (particularly relevant to locations with extremes of indoor or outdoor temperatures and humidity). For the average person who will outlay significant* *costs for his/her clothing each year, this system will achieve substantial economies and guarantee that person is well dressed at all times.'*

« »

I decided to interview BodyWare's spokesperson, and started checking who that might be. But the company proved to be elusive. I searched through various indexes and listings before finally coming across the name Sam Karvel whose 'corporate headquarters' were located at the bottom end of town, some distance from my own place.

I jumped into a self-drive cab and entered the address I had into the cab's keypad. The map showed a complex route to get there and I eventually found myself on a narrow street devoid of landscaping other than several clapped out petrol engine vehicles looking like they'd been abandoned decades ago. The footpaths and gutters were strewn with rubbish and animal excrement. As I searched for the right building, I ran the gauntlet of several homeless guys, sometimes accompanied by a hungry looking dog, hoping to cadge a few credits "for their fare home", as if they really had one.

A dingy six-storey building, at least 100 years old, was not where I might have expected to find the corporate headquarters for a game-changing invention. There were no signs on the front door, simply a few names listed next to the buzzer plate. I found a hand written entry for 'BodyWare' at last and pressed the entry buzzer. I tapped my foot waiting for some sign of life, then finally hearing a click, opened the door. I recoiled at the badly lit corridor leading to a steep stairway, and the faded carpet smelling strongly of cat-pee, dust and mould (to which I am strongly allergic). I fumbled for tissues as I went into a spasm of sneezing leaving me completely breathless.

With much huffing and puffing, I finally reached level four to see one of the doors ajar, projecting dim light over the dark corridor. As the creaking floor boards signalled my approach, the door opened slightly wider to reveal an elderly man waiting for me. He had a few straggles of grey hair. His face was shielded by thick-lensed spectacles and an unkempt beard. He had an unflinching stare, but I was distracted by the clothes he was wearing—garments that looked completely out of character—as though they might have been sourced from the pages of *FashBiz-Online*.

He didn't invite me in, keeping me at arm's length on his door step. I remained where I was, struggling to think what I should be asking him, while fumbling in my pocket to turn the media-matic to record without drawing his attention to what I was doing. "Mr Karvel, I publish an online science and technology news-digest and I was hoping to ask you some questions about your new invention as described in your recent patent application."

"So you just turned up, hoping to interview me without any warning?" His stare was a cross between angry and impatient, but mostly angry.

Journalism suits me best when I have some scope to review other people's work. And I'm particularly interested in game-changers, both the individuals responsible and the products they come up with. But this time I decided to play it cool and with a little scepticism, playing to the man's vanity before he ordered me to leave.

"Reading your patent application made me realise that if your claims are even halfway true, they will have a radical effect on certain industries, not the least of which are companies that sell clothing and all the suppliers of their raw products and equipment. They stand to lose, but you could make a fortune. Would you care to comment? Have you got a working prototype that I could see?"

Karvel looked at me as if I was an idiot. "Has it occurred to you that the clothes I'm wearing are of the finest quality, and not what you might have expected for a man of my age?"

I could see where he was heading, but equally I did not like being taken in. "You're not telling me that you're wearing this projected virtual clothing?"

He nodded in answer. My body language might have told him that I didn't believe a word of what he was saying. He smiled again, reaching behind his neck and fiddling with something. Suddenly he stood before me, now reduced to wearing a tightly fitting white cotton singlet and y-fronts, standing on plain plastic sandals. I gasped. "How did you do that?"

"That is my invention," he said smugly. "You've seen my patent application. The software and hardware are commercial-in-confidence, and will remain so. But by all means publish an article for your readers now that you have seen what it can do. Imagine this: there will be no limit to the style and quality of clothing that can be purchased by any individual who is willing to have their body scanned."

I was beginning to wonder whether he was either slightly deranged or a retired conjurer, and struggled to remember the questions I'd wanted to ask. "How much will all this cost, and are you set up to meet the demand for this invention which will be significant if what you are saying is true?"

He seemed to be weighing up the merits of confiding in me further before continuing. "I am not really concerned about the market demand because in all probability that will become the concern of others. But in the first instance I am setting the purchase price for my system at approximately the cost of one high fashion clothing set and one pair of shoes, totalling around US Credits 2000. Subsequent designs will be licensed for 50 credits apiece in this country and less in developing ones. Eventually there will be absolutely no competition from conventional clothing manufacturers, and the intelligent ones will be fighting each other to buy me out for the highest price they can command," he concluded with a self-satisfied curl of his lips.

We talked a little more and he permitted me to take before-and-after images of himself with a couple of his projected clothes designs. He promised to keep me in touch with developments and I in turn offered him a free subscription to my news-service.

« »

I left Karvel with conflicting thoughts buzzing around in my head, the foremost being concern for his safety if his claims could prove to be true. Surely he could not imagine that a whole sector of the economy would take an invention like this lying down! But then I reflected, who would have expected at the turn of the century what the invention of the smart phone would change? I recalled a prime example was the abandonment of film cameras. Companies which had manufactured colour film and the businesses in most retail centres which processed the film and prepared colour prints from the film, quickly disappeared.

Over the last 10 years, since 2040, I've been publishing my own science and technology news-service. I guess I have always been a 'wanabe scientist', the sort you see hunched over a test tube or a petri dish in a well-equipped lab, but I've never had the acute focus and persistence needed to uncover fresh discoveries over a great length of time. So I take some pride in the fact that once my piece on the BodyWare patent was published in my news-service, it quickly went into the stratosphere.

One after another, clothing companies and large retail chains made ill-informed negative statements concerning the invention and its risks ranging from skin cancer to hypothermia. Karvel despite arrogant confidence in his own management capabilities could not begin to meet the demand and was completely unprepared for the level of interest his invention generated, despite the inaccurate claims. Fake news items began to circulate including the most prevalent rumour that Karvel was connected with the PRC, the true originators of the patent, calculated to undermine the US economy.

I was forced to set my holo to filter all incoming calls "please leave TELNOTE detailing information you require and contact details."

The volume of TELNOTES grew and grew so quickly that I realised I'd have needed a secretary full time to respond to even the most interesting questions. By the end of the first week I was simply scanning and deleting most of them.

« »

Initially, the greatest demand for his virtual clothing system came from the lower end of the social ladder, appealing to those who could not afford anything approaching well designed clothing, let alone high fashion. But it didn't take long for a much broader segment of the population to see the attraction of the variety, quality and economy of garments available. They included actors, politicians, professionals and business people.

It also caught on with teenagers who in clear breach of the conditions of use shared their BodyWare system to camouflage themselves and play pranks on their mates. They started posting clips of each other being caught out over the internet. It quickly grew into a viral craze and for a brief time the opportunity to catch a BodyWare user in semi-nudity proved irresistible to a new population of voyeurs the world over. Public outrage when church clergymen and politicians were targeted led Karvel to issue a public apology. He also modified the system software with more sophisticated password protection and encryption to counteract the cyber-attacks.

On a more sinister level, one of my sources in the US-SECURE Agency called to let me know she'd been hearing rumours of BodyWare's potential for certain military applications. Not long after that Chester Trump, the grandson of Donald, a former US President, and in many ways a chip off the old block was tweeting his intention to sanction any country caught stealing the invention.

It simply went to prove my concern that Karvel had completely overlooked what should have been staring him in the face, most particularly his inability to cope with the level of interest and demand for his product. Halfway through the year the news feeds were announcing that a subsidiary of one of the largest tech companies in the United States saw its potential and made him an eight figure takeover offer, one which he could never hope to spend in his lifetime. Once the system had been streamlined and mass produced, the craze spread to an insatiable market from all corners of the globe, forcing any business that had been in the rag trade, and their associated design houses, either to licence BodyWare designs or go into liquidation.

« »

I had put aside my interest in BodyWare's corporate success, when I heard some intriguing reports on the grapevine about one 'Max' (Maximus) Kolon, a major player in the retail outlets most affected by the loss of market for their clothes. I did my research to discover that Max was an unusual individual who had equal measures of commercial know-how and scientific curiosity. The rumours were that he was also an ardent hacker, so good at it that he had once been contracted by a US Security Organisation to penetrate their most dangerous cyber opponents. There were also rumours that he'd been granted a special licence to reverse engineer the BodyWare system. The buzz was that he'd discovered something that was dynamite for defence. So given his new defence/security status it was with considerable difficulty that I was eventually able to meet him.

Kolon was of average height with thinning ginger hair. He was unprepossessing with the dishevelled look that his clothes had been sourced from the used section of the laundry basket. Significantly, I realised he was not using BodyWare himself. He had a perpetually furtive expression, and was forever adding to a sentence: "You know what I mean don't you?" It had taken me quite some time and I had to pull a lot of strings to arrange an interview with the man because, as he told me, the nature of his work put him in the sights of the main spy agencies, and he needed to stay undercover as much as possible. I didn't quite understand what he meant, but he put up a hand as I started to ask.

"I'm not quite clear why you wanted this interview?" he said.

"I read that your textile design company was one of the casualties of BodyWare. I am following up a couple of cases like yours to better understand the implications of BodyWare on a whole sector of our economy. Would you mind answering a few questions?"

Max thought for a minute, then shrugged his shoulders dismissively. "Well I suppose I can answer a couple of questions, but obviously reserve the right to make no further comment."

"How long did it take you to realise that BodyWare was here to stay, and the effect it would have on your business?"

"Too long, far too long! If I'd realised how quickly the market would change, I would have taken action much sooner." He paused to take a sip of water and contemplate what he hadn't done. "Have you met the original guy who is responsible for BodyWare?" he asked.

I didn't want to admit my sources so I gave him a noncommittal answer: "I had a brief contact with him, but he didn't seem to have any idea of the implications of his invention."

"I'm going to tell you something, so that you understand how significant the BodyWare system really is. I don't even think that even now Karvel has realised its full potential."

"That wouldn't surprise me," I said. "He is what you might describe as a boffin, and an eccentric one at that. I formed the opinion that he was quite naive and didn't realise that if his invention was as effective as he claimed, the reaction on him would be far more than he realised. He didn't seem to realise that he would almost certainly be putting his life at risk."

Rodney Jensen

"That doesn't really surprise me," said Max with a nod. "The thing he hasn't realised is that quite apart from clothing, it has many potential applications, for example for camouflaging uniforms and the outside surfaces of buildings and infrastructure. It's much simpler and cheaper to project a camouflage design onto a surface than to paint it, and it can be one that is dynamic rather than static, ripples on water for ships, for example. So naturally the defence forces, who have generous budgets to spend on camouflage, are huge potential customers for BodyWare. Of course it goes much further than that. They want not only to control the commercial in confidence aspects of the invention, but also to make sure applications like special dynamic camouflage don't fall into potential enemy hands."

By now I was beginning to get the drift of what Max was telling me, but I still wasn't quite getting what role he was playing. "So what is your interest in all this?" I asked him.

He smiled slightly and shrugged his shoulders. "I'm afraid that's a 'no comment', and I'm sure that you can guess why, given what I've just told you."

"So who holds the key to BodyWare right now? As far as I'm aware there was a takeover by another corporation. Does US defence have a say in all of this?"

"Quite obviously they have a say and it's a big one. I'm not going to tell you what my involvement is or what defence are doing since they're both classified."

« »

Word got out that Chester Trump was booked to address the UN about the latest trade sanctions against the Middle East, Mexico, South America, China and others, including Korea and Turkey. He was particularly fired up by recent Chinese efforts to hack into and steal various US defence systems. The reason for his special presentation was that cyber-security for BodyWare was becoming an extremely high priority. Little did we realise that the reason for his campaign was not simply a matter of maintaining a commercial/trade advantage.

I managed to procure an observer ticket to attend his address on the basis of a couple of lies about my status and my press card. When I arrived, the UN Chamber was packed to capacity with press representatives eager to hear the US President making an address in person.

The audience hushed as Chester Trump ascended the lectern, flanked by three armed bodyguards. His dress was BodyWare perfect as were the uniforms of his bodyguards. He was a practiced orator and took his time getting his papers straight, then staring out the audience before he began his opening words.

"My friends and colleagues of the UN. I welcome you to this gathering and an opportunity for me to share something which is deeply disturbing, not only to my country but to me personally." There was a long pause as the audience fell completely silent, contemplating what must be so important for the President to be making waves.

"Firstly I have to point the finger at some of you sitting before me. Yes you who have blatantly engaged in what is politely known as cyber-crime on our country's defence systems and associated corporations. We know and you know who you are."

As he said this, Trump was staring pointedly at the PRC, Iranian, Korean and Russian spokespersons. Each of them was trying hard to remain expressionless, despite their body language saying otherwise. They seemed to be squirming beneath the onslaught of the President's finger wagging. "And BodyWare," he continued, "has not simply been the focus of our commercial opponents, but also our strategic interests. As I speak, we are about to identify those who have been foremost ..."

Trump halted in mid-sentence as he realised something was wrong. There had been a loud gasp from his audience, followed by excited chatter and one loud voice saying "They've got nothing on!" Trump looked over his shoulders shocked to see that his bodyguards were in their underwear, and glancing down at his own body, he could see himself in the same state.

Then there was an even greater wave of shock and now fear as the President and his three bodyguards winked out of existence. Reporters were frantically playing back their vid recordings to check what had happened. There was a hubbub of anxious voices and many were screaming and crying in panic. One of the government officials tried to take control via the microphone, but nobody was taking any notice of his vain efforts to calm them down.

I ran out of the press gallery to file my story, at least as soon if not before other mainstream media sources. Having done that, I scanned the Net to discover that it was generally believed a hacker had managed to infiltrate the BodyWare software and apply a projection of impenetrable black on selected subjects. If you looked in their direction, all you could see was a black silhouette as though you were peering into a deep hole. My fellow journalists were not slow to see the amazing strategic advantage of this new discovery, which could be applied to various vehicles of war such as armoured cars, tanks, airplanes and men themselves. It was not simply the camouflage that Max Kolon had alluded to. It was virtual invisibility that could make a plane, a vehicle or a person, or anything for that matter, impossible to detect visually.

It was also pretty obvious that whoever had done this could not have chosen a better time to embarrass the US President and his entire country. He or she might on the one hand be seen as a whistle-blower intent on balancing the arms race, or "a damned traitor", as Chester Trump fumed once his system had been re-booted and was almost back to normal. Personally I suspected that Max Kolon had somehow been involved in disrobing and then blanking out the President but was never able to prove it. After this sensational event, few others wished to continue taking that risk. Within a week BodyWare Corporation had been served with legal notices and demands for refunds, given its vulnerability to sabotage. The company went into liquidation before the year was out, having surrendered the entire BodyWare system to the Government, where it remained top secret and sealed in perpetuity. There was a resurgence in the clothing industry and a gamut of new fashions hit the streets. The poor who had not been wealthy enough to invest in a BodyWare system, continued their lives as if nothing had happened.

« »

Rodney Jensen

Reference for Tale 8

This story is based on Hans Andersen's well known tale 'The Emperor's New Clothes' in which two crafty rogues pretend that they have developed a textile that remains invisible for anyone unfit for the office they hold. The Emperor cannot admit in front of his courtiers that he is unable to see this magical cloth, and they of course also pretend they can see it. On the day of a great procession in which the Emperor is dressed in his fake finery, it takes an innocent boy to shout out "he's wearing no clothes!" whereupon everyone else realizes they've been tricked.

Tale 9: Cinderella

I'm sitting on the front veranda of my property at Bendoogal sipping a glass or two of an excellent wine I've been keeping for a special occasion. It's a beautiful autumn evening, not a cloud in the sky, aromatic scents of eucalypts from nearby woodlands and the calls of many birds local and migratory, all uniquely Australian. Even the buzzing sound of my Ag-Drone, flying high over my roof on its way to the new orchard close to the creek line, is comforting rather than annoying because without it and other technology we now use, we would never have survived in this part of rural Australia.

I'm feeling a tad sentimental for the traditional farm we once had. It's my 60th birthday and I've been reflecting on the many changes needed to make it viable today. So my celebration is not so much because I'm hitting a big milestone, but the success we've had in turning the place around. I haven't had an easy life and

Rodney Jensen

I've encountered many obstacles since my early childhood.

What life does not have its occasional setbacks? I'm sure most do, but I think mine stands out. I'm not bitter, but neither am I easily able to forget the source of some of my 'growing pains'.

« »

My birth was at a time when IVF had become the norm for couples who'd postponed having a family until their late 30s for economic reasons, then discovering too late that natural conception was difficult, if impossible to accomplish. That is probably what happened with my parents who in my eyes seemed very old. It's almost certain that IVF was why I was born one of three triplets. I was named 'Cinderella' doubtless a flight of fancy but forever onwards 'Cindy'. My two brothers were named 'Matt' and 'Wiley'.

As we grew older it became obvious that both my parents were conventional in so many ways including gender-bias, where prejudice was there but taken for granted. For example, we all had our share of chores around the property and my mother automatically assumed that because I was the girl, I should take the entire responsibility for keeping our bedrooms tidy, making the beds, cleaning the bathroom and sweeping the floors. It would never have occurred to my parents to buy one of the new bot-cleaners instead of expecting me to slave away like my fairy tale namesake. Similarly, my father was still driving a diesel ute nearly 40 years old and a Ferguson tractor that should have been kept in a museum.

My father was just as biased about me as mum was. I'll always remember the time I came off a horse while racing with him and my brothers around the family racing track. Instead of stopping, the three of them continued with their circuit and when we re-grouped and the others were laughing about the mud and grass on my face and clothes. I cried, "I could have broken my neck for all you care!" My anger was heightened as I remembered the fuss he and my mother had made about Wiley coming off his horse about three months before. They even called a doctor to check him out for fractures. Boys were clearly so much more important on the farm than girls.

Dad, who refused to admit any serious concern for what had happened to me, remained unrepentant. He remarked: "You're a far better rider than that, you'll be okay." And that was it. End of story.

In our teenage years we siblings became more competitive at high school, though I generally got better results than both my brothers despite all the extra chores I was expected to do. I was proudly boasting about my art grades for which I had A's, while Matt and Wiley both scraped C's from our art teacher 'Macksy'. Matt could not resist pulling me down a peg or two by calling me 'teacher's pet', then remarking: "He always loves everything you do, can't imagine why!" At which point I knee'd him in the balls. Unfortunately both my parents were around and heard the ruckus. I was punished because of the moaning and carrying on Matt made. I had my holo confiscated for a week. I tried hard to suppress my anger about this. Losing my holo's contact with the outside world was no small penalty. I felt it was grossly unfair given the provocation.

And so our childhood progressed. It became something of a pattern with my school results nearly always being a shade better than my two brothers, despite still bearing the brunt of the housework while the boys were let off farm work to study. It never occurred to them that perhaps I worked harder than they did. The thing which really brought matters to a head was in creative writing. We learned from our online English Studies program that the state's education department was offering prizes for short stories on any subject up to 5000 words. We all had a go at putting our imagination into stories. Just in case either Matt or Wiley tried to steal my ideas, I deliberately saved what I thought was a really badly thought-out piece of work in a prominently located folder named 'short story competition', while my actual entry was hidden under a much more obscure label, and password protected just to satisfy my paranoia. Whether or not either of them succeeded in accessing the dummy entry or not I never knew. I didn't get to see their entries, neither of them got a mention, but I got a special award for writing about life on a small farm in country New South Wales. Instead of seeming impressed Wiley remarked, "think yourself so smart don'tcha!" and Matt sniggered as I ran out of the room.

At the time the three of us were half way through our final year of secondary education, our lives took an unexpected turn. My father began complaining of abdominal pains and made several trips to our local GP, followed up by a trip to a specialist in North Sydney. He was sent off for a CT scan and then received a death sentence. He had pancreatic cancer, was given less than twelve months to live and died in six. So there were the three of us siblings with mum on the farm which dad had barely kept afloat, faced with the impossible dilemma of what we should do next.

For several months the world seemed to be in suspension, and we all found it difficult to focus. We managed somehow to get through our exams at the end of the year. Our results were not outstanding, but in theory sufficient to gain university entrance. My mother was now faced with us heading off to university and having not only to keep the household afloat but also the farm. Dad had been entirely responsible for the farm work and it was more than a full time job. We had all tried to help out once our secondary studies were completed, but it clearly wasn't working. Mum had grown grey-white, not only with her hair, but also in her mental state.

We had a crisis conference shortly after Christmas that year. The discussion confirmed something I had already worked out, that for any of us wanting to attend university, we were facing an economic precipice. Our results weren't good enough to gain any financial assistance. Our household income was too small to pay for board. Then there was the question of what would happen to mum if we all left home. Someone should stay to keep the farm afloat and become mum's carer. My school results were by far the best, and as I had been less involved in the work on the farm, I was hardly in a position to manage it on my own. However the others seemed to have automatically assumed the person to stay would be me, until I dropped my bombshell.

"I've already enrolled at UNE for Ag Science. I will be deferring fees until I've graduated and paying my board by working weekends and Friday nights."

My mother and brothers were dumbfounded and angry. I was labelled self-centred and uncaring. I packed my things and was off the next day.

I remained in purgatory for nearly a year and despite several efforts to contact mum, I got minimal responses from her. When I did eventually get to see her again she was slightly mollified by the fact I'd been awarded a scholarship which enabled me to send a few dollars home to her each week, to help out on the farm. From then on, I did visit my mum whenever I could, and established a far better relationship with her than I had as a teenager. But I didn't see my brothers until more than three years later.

« »

I'd organized a party to celebrate finishing my course with honours. While honours meant I could have gone on to do a PhD, more practical research was in my sights. As a sort of peace offering and despite having been ignored repeatedly I yet again invited my brothers to come along with their partners, neither of whom I'd met. I shut my mind to the considerable risk of mixing my celebration with family introductions. There was every prospect of it being an awkward first time meeting with two females who, in all probability, had only heard of me by disrepute. There was also the potential for tension with my brothers. But I threw caution to the wind. In addition to my 'special guests', I invited as many friends as could possibly be squeezed into the tiny cottage my flat-mate and I had been sharing. It was a short distance from the UNE campus in Armidale.

It was late in November when we held the bash, nearly everyone I had invited was there, including the neighbours, lest they complain about the noise. I was out in the street welcoming people, when two strange men with women in tow emerged from a self-drive. They were dressed to kill making us all looked like a shabby underclass in our jeans and T-shirts. Christ! They were Matt and Wiley seemingly mature and respectable! My other friends stared at them as though they'd walked in from outer space. I greeted them, not knowing quite what to do—a peck on the cheek, a token hug?

Matt did hug me like he meant it. Wiley gave me a reserved kiss, then came the introductions.

"I'm Ella," said the tall willowy blonde at Matt's shoulder, "but call me 'Ells', all our mates do." She squeezed my hand, like she thought of me as a tragic. I was particularly taken by her crimson lipstick and matching nail polish and the strong waft of *Mon Amour* perfume. *What does she have to feel sympathetic about?*

"I'm Cindy," I said unnecessarily, touched her hand and turned to Wiley's partner, who was quite intense looking, with heavy rimmed spectacles framing her face, and wearing a formal looking pantsuit. I smiled at her and we briefly pecked each other's cheeks. "Rachel," she said and smiled.

Of the two partners, I was the more intimidated by Rachel, based on her reputation. My mum had mentioned she worked in the New South Wales Premier's Department as one of the State Minister's advisors. *What would she make of my humble group of new grads in Ag. Science? And whatever can she see in Wiley!*

Wiley, now being in real estate, had invited a potential investor who was visiting from Indonesia. "This is 'Wy'," said my brother, when Wy arrived halfway through the evening. "Wy is on a short visit to interview some of our property experts, and I've been showing him some of the apartments on our books." Wy looked like he didn't really want to talk about property investment, but mentioned one of his Indonesian friends at UNE was doing a PhD on the Australian property market. He seemed relaxed and smart. His English was very good. "My name is short for 'Wayan' and I'm from Bali, but I went to the International School in Jakarta," he explained.

I immediately decided I quite fancied Wy. He seemed a good deal more sophisticated than my brothers. "Can I get you a drink?" I asked him.

"Yes please, as long as it's non-alcoholic." I must have looked slightly bemused given the litres of alcohol sloshed down by my friends. "It's not that I don't drink alcohol," he said seriously, "but I am recovering from a bout of malaria and it is not really good for my liver."

"Not a problem," I said, "I should cut down myself."

As parties go, it was quite enjoyable, despite my having the responsibilities of being a host. I really liked Wy, who was above average good looks and unlike many Indonesian men, comparatively tall. I was disappointed to learn he'd be returning to Indonesia the following day, recalled by the research organisation he was working for.

"What a shame, how can I contact you then?" I said with a fake laugh to disguise the fact that I was really interested in renewing the acquaintance.

"I didn't bring a card," he said. "But your brother has my contact details. I'd be delighted to meet you again next time I'm down here." And that was the last I saw of him.

« »

I see that party as being something of a turning point in the relationship with my brothers who had changed dramatically since childhood. Both had gone into money-making jobs after completing their secondary education, rather than struggling through university as I had. Both were successful in their own right. Matt now worked for a high pressure stockbroking company in Sydney. Wiley had become a salesman with an online real estate business. Neither had stayed to work the farm. Mum was still at the homestead under the watchful eyes of our neighbours, but the farm had been left to deteriorate.

At the party there was too much noise for a meaningful reunion and my brothers seemed to inhabit a very different commercial world from my university environment. I'm not sure what exactly the two of them thought of me. The intimacy and the rivalry we'd shared as triplet children seemed to have changed to more overt dislike, mixed with incomprehension and disdain.

Matt as he was leaving, said: "So where do you see yourself in the next five years?" or some such mindless psycho-babble that I didn't deign to reply to and just laughed. Matt and Ella left shortly after. Her perfume lingered for days afterwards.

Wiley did at least manage to show some slight interest in what I'd been studying, and asked me what I was planning to do with my new qualifications.

"I'm intending to go back to the farm and treat it as a project," I said.

He looked bemused. "Really? Well at least you can look after mum then. Have you thought of the possibility that we can sell the property? We can put mum in a home where she belongs and you'll be free. That would be best all round wouldn't it?"

I was shocked and disappointed by this response. It sounded like he'd completely washed his hands of mum and the farm, although I couldn't really criticise him having made a university education my own priority. "I don't think so, I have other ideas," I finally responded, and left it at that.

I didn't at that stage want to telegraph the radical approach I'd envisaged for turning what had become a financial liability into a sustainable and prosperous enterprise. But I did call Wiley the next day to ask him if he could give me Wy's contact details. He seemed curiously reticent. "His email never works and I've got his phone number written down somewhere. I'll get back to you if I can find it."

I knew Wiley well enough to be certain this was a blatant lie. So I was not surprised when he never did get back to me, and I didn't get to understand *what was his*

Rodney Jensen

problem? Could it be because Wy was Indonesian? Surely not! I would never have thought of Wiley as racist. Was there something about Wy he was aware of that he was trying to protect me from?

Much later I was to discover that my brothers had formed a building company using our family name and called it 'Cummings Property'. They started building speculative houses on the outskirts of Sydney, generally making a 30 percent profit on sales. They grew rapidly and over time turned to larger high rise housing developments. Had I understood better how the two of them had gone about financing their enterprise, it might have saved me a great deal of heartache.

« »

Shortly after graduation I returned home, motivated by a combination of guilt about mum's state of health and a desire to put the property back on track. Mum had started suffering occasional fainting fits, and wasn't able to do even the most basic periodic maintenance needed on our property. In the few years I had been at university it had become seriously overgrown with weeds, wattle and eucalypt saplings in the process of natural regeneration. Left alone it could soon return to native forest, and part of me was tempted to let that happen. However if I was ever to make the farm viable, I had to find a balance between natural regeneration and my farm improvement plans. That was if I intended to make a living or be able to keep mum at home.

My objectives for the property were firstly to minimise environmental stress from the farming practices we adopted, and secondly, to achieve a reasonable financial return. Sounded simple, but if that were so, many more would have been doing it rather than simply walking off their properties when their money ran out.

By now, mum had started treating me as an adult who should be listened to and did not attempt to interfere in my plans. When I began to explain what I was thinking, she only said, "I've got confidence in whatever you do girl."

While I had lots of ideas of my own I still sought advice from one or two of my most respected academics at UNE and some of the local farmers who'd already abandoned traditional approaches in favour of new farming technology, and seemed to be succeeding.

Initially I did not see how I could possibly turn the farm around single-handed and manage mum. One of my advisors helped me to realise that I could not continue without a substantial injection of money. I paid a visit to the local bank with a feasibility study including projected costs and returns over a five year period signed off by my accountant. There was a lot of negotiation over the finance, but eventually I got my loan with above market interest rates and a binding agreement to demonstrate reasonable financial progress within 12 months and profitability within 2 years.

With access to funds at last, I interviewed a series of qualified nurse-carers to take care of mum full-time on the property. Funding her care would immediately absorb 25% of my loan without contributing anything to the return the bank was after. The second thing I did was to invite my university to become involved in my experimental farming program, specially tailored for this marginal region. In exchange for the university participation, I would offer to fund a postdoctoral member of staff to review and evaluate options for turning things around.

« »

Rodney Jensen

Not long after the confirmation of the loan, and I had finished for the day and was just settling down to have a beer in our lounge, I heard the sound of an approaching vehicle. I went to the door to see who it was and met a formally dressed man carrying a briefcase.

"I spoke to your mother two days ago and understand you are now in charge of this property?" I nodded, thinking that mother forgetting to pass on such a call was not unusual.

"Would you mind if I come inside. There is something I need to discuss with you."

I said nothing but led him into our kitchen and sat him down at the large kitchen table. My mother was upstairs taking a nap and I decided to leave her undisturbed. The man pulled open his briefcase and pulled out a document. "Miss Cummings, I have a copy of your contract here that you, your mother and your brothers have signed with the NSW Rural Bank five years ago."

I was confused thinking that he must be getting his wires mixed over the loan I had just secured from the bank to help me develop my plan for the farm. Then I realised it was me who was mistaken, because my loan was not with the NSW Rural Bank but the Australian Investment Bank where I had had a personal account during my time in Armidale. He picked up the document flipped to the last page and showed it to me. There were four names countersigned with signatures. I was stunned to see that my name and signature was there next to my two brothers and mother.

"That's not my signature, and that one doesn't look like my mother's" I said

"Yes it is. All the signatures have been witnessed by a Justice of the Peace. If it isn't yours, how do you explain that?"

"I've no idea. Someone must have forged my signature. But there's a Justice of the Peace involved, I have no explanation for that!" My voice was becoming shrill and I realised I must calm down and try to work out what had been going on. I could already see my brothers' hands all over this. "What does this contract say?" I asked.

"The contract is for a loan of $1.5 million secured by this property the deeds of which we are holding."

I was shaking with a mixture of fear and rage wondering how my brothers had managed to take possession of the deeds. It must have been mum. *Maybe they convinced her that they should be put in safe custody with a bank* I thought grimly. *She wouldn't have thought that suspicious. Why should she?*

"But I'm afraid there is more I have to tell you." By the tone of his voice I had a sick feeling and I could guess what was coming.

"Under this fixed interest contract, your brothers are obliged to make monthly payments of $7500 per month. The bank has received no payments into their loan account for six months and under the terms of the contract we are entitled to take possession of this property and put it up for sale."

"Now?" I whispered aghast.

"Miss Cummings. The Bank I represent has generously agreed to present you and your family with a 4 week's grace-period to make up the interest payments and charges you owe the Bank. Failure to do that will result in an eviction notice being issued. The Bank will take possession of this property and auction it to the highest bidder. Here is my card, please contact me to let me know what you have decided?"

I led the man to the door not knowing what to say. He paused on the threshold and looked at me sympathetically as I brushed my eyes. "Miss Cummings, if what you have said just now is the truth I would strongly advise you to find a lawyer. Secondly, you will need to think carefully as to any evidence you can find to support your claim that it is not you and your mother's signatures on the contract."

Two weeks had passed and Mum and I were no nearer to finding the huge amount of money to cover the debt my brothers had racked up. I spoke to Matt and Wiley, but they had little to say, other than to admit they were bankrupt and their company had gone into liquidation when the 2032 property bubble finally burst.

"How dare you use this property as collateral for your business without asking me and forging my and mum's signature?" I shouted.

"We effectively own half of it whether you like it or not. And Mum signed it even though she doesn't remember. Anyway when Mum's gone it will be two thirds. If you stop pestering us, Wiley and I might scrape together a bit of compensation for you but if you try taking this to court you'll end up with nothing," was Matt's response.

My mother had been quite poorly for a while and was just into her 70's. She had been suffering a sequence of 'turns' as she called them and then one day I came back into the homestead and found her on the floor unconscious with a dribble of saliva in the corner of her mouth. The ambulance took an interminable time to come and she was pronounced dead on arrival at the hospital.

I never got to discuss properly with her what my brothers had done, including tricking her into signing the contract. But with hindsight I felt relieved that I hadn't been forced to disillusion her about the two boys she had adored throughout their childhood.

With Mum gone, I took my brothers to Court, and was forced to run the case myself without any legal support, because I simply couldn't afford it.

The Court Case was held six months later, and the day started with a protracted examination of the facts of the case. As it turned out, my brothers and the bent JP had been careless with their forgery. In particular there was an issue with the date of the agreement that was shown on the contract. What they couldn't have known was that the date of all the signatures happened to be at the same time Mum and I were at an interstate conference on 'Farming for the Future'. I had taken mum with me for company and we were able to prove our attendance at the Conference and our three nights stay at a Gold Coast Motel.

I advised the Bank of this evidence of forgery and they joined my action as plaintiffs in the hearing and brought along an eminent barrister to represent their case. The Judge stopped the proceedings on the first day set down, sternly rebuked my brothers for perjury and fraud and handed down an eighteen month prison sentence with parole after a year. The Justice of the Peace (whom I discovered was a close friend of both my brothers) was also hauled over the coals and given a three year sentence for his part in the fraud, deemed to be worse taking into consideration his position of public responsibility.

In his findings, the Judge further decided that given their fraudulent conduct in respect to me and my late mother, my brothers had forfeited their right to make any claim whatsoever on me for the farm or future farm proceeds.

I have never seen either of my brothers since that harrowing day in Court. The contract with the bank was deemed null and void and it was left to the Bank to take separate proceedings against them for recovery of unpaid interest.

« »

With the help of my advice from the Uni, I'd been struggling on the farm, when life took yet another unexpected turn. I was in the large covered vegetable beds of my new aquaponic plant close to our homestead, when I heard a vehicle coming up the driveway. I carried on with my work thinking it was a delivery but I turned to see a casually dressed bearded man coming through into the enclosure and standing across the bed from where I was working. I was about to tell him that he should leave immediately (foreign bodies and contamination of nutrients are a perennial issue with a large scale aquaponic system) when I realised with a start that it was Wy.

"Good heavens, what are you doing here!" the words rushed out of my mouth without the normal filtering process, as I was feeling flustered.

Wy smiled warmly. "I have come to see you, especially as you never got back to me." Seeing the puzzled look on my face he added "you made no use of the contact details I left with your brother?"

"You mean Wiley? He didn't give me your details."

"Hmmm, come to think of it he just put my card in his pocket. He did surprise me by not seeming the least interested in the fact that I was wanting to contact you. In my own family, anyone wanting to visit my sister would probably have to be vetted by my father first, and in his absence by me. Although I must admit we are becoming slightly more relaxed about such matters these days." He laughed lightly.

"Well that's a relief," I said, still coming to terms with what was increasingly sounding like the guy was as interested in me as I'd felt about him at the party.

The conversation hung for a few beats as we both stared at each other.

"Would you like me to show you around, now that you've come all this way?" I said this as brightly as I could, wondering what this virtual stranger, an urban property investor, could possibly find of interest here. *Did he know anything about farming or recent innovative technology?*

He seemed so serious, like he was on a mission and that made me even more nervous.

"I would love you to show me around," he smiled making me feel slightly more at ease. "I know you have not been to Indonesia and no doubt you would be surprised how different our farming ways are to yours. I am sure there will be much to learn from what you are doing here. I hope you do not mind if I ask you many questions?"

"Ask what you like," I said shyly. *Was this guy for real?*

« »

Wy ended up spending three days on my property. He was fascinated with what I was trying to do, particularly with the extensive use of AI and drones to monitor ground conditions and adjust the extensive drip irrigation system that kept the orchards optimally watered. At times I felt he really was more interested in my farming systems than he was in me. I had mixed feelings about the fact that he had made no attempt at any physical advances or nocturnal visitations from his bedroom to mine. Had he done so I doubt whether I would have put up much resistance.

Rodney Jensen

Finally, when the time came for him to leave and catch his return flight to Bali, I could not help feeling a pang of disappointment that he could not stay longer. The one thing that did make me hope it would not be the last I would be seeing of him was his promise to arrange for me to meet his family in Bali. *Crikey that sounds ominous!*

« »

Eventually Wy was to keep his promise and invited me to visit him and his family in Bali. I had never visited Indonesia before and was enchanted by the richness and colour of the Hindu culture. Wy had several sisters and one younger brother. I did my best to make friends, particularly with his sisters, although they were a lot younger than me, but I guessed they might have a strong influence on Wy regarding his matchmaking. Less than two days after my arrival he asked me whether I would marry him. I gave him my answer without the slightest hesitation.

"We think it would be best if we host the wedding here in Bali, so that we can have a Hindu ceremony?" Again I had no reservations about this.

« »

Now that it's growing dark, I must stop this indulgent contemplation and get myself ready for this evening's celebrations. My life with Wy and our children has been a period of great happiness. Wy is still in the shower and will be joining me soon for a drink. Then we're heading off to Armidale to meet some of our friends and my two grown up children to help us celebrate this 60th birthday. I cannot believe how quickly the years have passed by.

It did take longer than we had estimated for us to turn the farm into an ongoing and financially viable operation. Nowadays it earns more than enough for us to continue implementing new AI systems and the whole thing runs like clockwork with very little human intervention.

Wy now has a teaching post at UNE and takes his students on field trips up to Bali to help his fellow Balinese implement systems similar to those we use here. I sometimes also lecture the post grads in Ag Science. My classes are always well attended.

« »

Reference for Tale 9

This story relates to the very famous 'Cinderella' of Grimms' Fairy Tales. Cinderella has the misfortune to lose her mother at a young age; then her father chooses to marry a spiteful woman with two ugly daughters who treat Cinderella as their skivvy. When her three in-laws do

Rodney Jensen

everything in their power to prevent her from attending a ball with the King and his handsome Prince, Cinderella's kindness to her friends the birds is rewarded with beautiful clothes. She attends the ball, and tries to evade the Prince's attention, who eventually finds and marries her.

For the ugly step-sisters I have substituted uncaring triplet brothers and set a more futuristic path for my heroine. Her handsome Prince who eventually helps to save her from her brothers is an Indonesian property investor, who has hoped to make his fortune in Australia and finds her instead.

« »

Tale 10: The Princess and the Pea

'I was in the first shortlisted group for the Mars mission that Musk was planning in the 2020s before another consortium bought him out. Do you remember the 'First Habitat Mission' or were you too young to remember much about that?"

Nat is the first person I've ever shared my story with, other than my partner. Nat has been serving customers in this North Sydney Bar which by now is empty, apart from me nursing my drink in a corner. He walks over, carrying a drink for himself in one hand and another for me, one I haven't ordered. He politely asks whether I mind him joining me, as he's closing the bar for the evening.

My revelation about the Mars mission wasn't meant to shock him, but it has certainly caught his attention. Being a barman he's not exactly shy, and this first time we meet, he seems a bit underwhelming. But when he explains he is working his way through college to become an accredited journalist, I think that perhaps there is more to him than I've given credit for. So we continue our chat and I feel the least I can do is to seem grateful for his drink on the house.

I don't exactly remember how I got to this point of telling him about the latest efforts to send a spaceship to the stars. Actually there is still a strict blanket on ANY discussion about the Musk Planetary and Stellar Missions with outsiders. But tonight, having recently gone through a torrid break-up with my longstanding partner Marg, I'm really feeling the need to talk with someone whom I probably will never see again—someone who seems sympatico and not likely to be on his holo tomorrow with 'Behind the Scenes' or some such chat media.

Of course he obviously wants to know a lot more. "It was easily the most challenging time in my life, and I've had a few of those," I continue.

Nat is a good listener. He simply takes a sip of his drink and leans back in his seat waiting for me to continue. I take a deep breath. "Actually the biggest thing that ever happened to me was finding out something about myself from my parents. Sadly they are long gone now, but they were decent people and felt I had a right to know this fact as soon as I was grown up enough to understand."

Nat remains in listening mode, encouraging me to continue.

"I still remember that morning as though it were yesterday. It was my tenth birthday. They had bought me a new bicycle, it was red and shiny, I couldn't wait to take it outside for a trial ride. But it was raining and my Dad said that it would be better to wait for a sunny day and we could all go out to a park with it.

"In my eyes both he and my Mum seemed a lot older than my friends' parents. They also seemed a lot more deliberate about everything, the opposite of the spontaneous and funny ways I saw in other parents.

"On that birthday morning Dad was looking especially thoughtful and my Mum was more nervous than happy as I might have expected. They asked me to come and sit down with them in the living room. 'Mama and I have something to tell you Celine,' my Dad began. Both my parents still spoke precise and accented English quite different from other parents in my suburb. I knew this was because they were living in Denmark before I was born and migrated to Australia with me as a baby. As most Danish people do, they spoke English fluently, but their accent had still not left them after ten years in Australia."

"We sat down and there was an awkward silence. Neither Mum nor Dad seemed to know how to begin or what to say. Finally Dad broke the silence. 'Celine, you know that you were born in Denmark?' I nodded my head. 'Well there is something else we have never told you.' He was talking softly and had a strange expression, kind of happy and sad at the same time. I waited patiently for him to continue. 'The truth is that you were born to other parents, and they decided it would be best to give you to us. I am sure that they loved you as much as we do, and must have had a good reason to do what they did. And of course we love you just as much as if you were born to us.' He was trying to smile, but amazingly he seemed to be tearing up. It was something I had never seen before."

" 'We felt that you should know this,' my Mum chimed in, 'now that you are so grown up you can understand what we are telling you.' She tried to make it sound a bit jokey, but I was feeling amazed and confused. I asked them to tell me more about my real parents, but they said that it would be best for me not to know, because they wouldn't want me to try to contact them."

"By this time I was in tears. The pleasure of my new bike had evaporated with the sense that my pretend parents had been lying to me all this time. When they steadfastly refused to give me any further information I became hysterical, ran to my room and locked the door. I did not come out until lunchtime and my parents would add no more to what they'd said other than evasive remarks like: 'it can wait until you are 18, when you can make your own mind up about what to do'."

I come back to earth and realise Nat has been listening patiently as I have recollected all this. "I never could understand why they absolutely refused to explain what happened, leaving me with a new sense of insecurity that would dog my childhood. Then they were both killed in a car accident and it was left to me to try to discover why I had been sourced from somewhere in Copenhagen."

"Does this have anything to do with the Mars team?" Nat asks thoughtfully.

"Yes it does. After my parents' revelation, I began to see myself as different from everyone else at school. I never told anyone that I was adopted. I had to prove that I was just as good as everyone else and worked twice as hard at school work and sports."

"Do you think your parents understood what was going on?"

"No ... but I think they were pleased when I started coming first at everything. They didn't really understand why, and perhaps I didn't myself. But the fact was that my growing obsession to be best at everything was born of a terrible sense of being different, together with the unanswered question of why my original parents had abandoned me."

Nat nods, and surprises me with his next insightful question. "So you became interested in the toughest stuff school can throw at you?"

"That's right Nat—maths, physics, biology. Apart from classes, I soaked up everything I could, studying for hours online and ended up knowing more about the subject matter than my teachers, much to their annoyance!" I laugh remembering how most of them reacted to being corrected by a teenager.

"By the time I'd finished high school I had a scholarship to attend Sydney University and completed a PhD in astrophysics by the time I was 25."

« »

Nat listens with growing interest as I recounted how I became obsessed with being one of the first colonists to Mars.

"All of us who applied to be colonists were informed that it would be a one-way journey to the planet and the supply of provisions from Earth would last only until the first habitat had been completed. After that we were expected to be self-sufficient or perish. Despite this there was no shortage of candidates. Even after the shortlisting, I was competing for a place with fifty others. The lucky few who were awarded a place on the mission, were destined to become the first humans to take up temporary accommodation on the surface of Mars."

"Yes I've read and heard about the problems the habitat approach encountered when it was realized that hurricane force winds and prolonged dust storms had been totally underestimated and the approach had to be reassessed," Nat remarked.

"You must have watched the same mini-series that everyone else has seen, documenting the difficulties of

Rodney Jensen

getting established on Mars. Our planners *had* realised our first priority would be to find a more practicable habitat than the inflatable structure that was planned as the interim step. Longer term it was hoped that the habitat would be built deep in an underground cavern (most likely a former volcanic vent) where an abundance of ice would enable it to be self-sufficient in food, water and air.

"Back to the selection process I had to go through, we all had to rely entirely on the same synthetic meals we would have on Mars. The meals proved to be my undoing."

Nat looks at me with renewed interest. "They can't have been that bad surely?"

"You'd be surprised how they can affect you. There's a terrible sameness and lack of variety you have to live with. The solid foods taste particularly awful. Whether it's a scrambled meat formulation based on soy proteins or biscuits made from strands of seaweed. The drinks aren't quite so bad, but I generally preferred to stick to recycled water, trying not to dwell too much on its origins."

"Surely there were worse things than that to deal with?"

"I am sure there would have been worse things to come, but as I'm about to explain, I never did get to be tested at the higher selection levels. I probably could have hidden how much I hated the food and drink, but somehow others were noticing. Maybe I talked too much with people I mistakenly trusted. Anyway it got around with the others."

"They used it against you?"

"They used it against me for sure."

In my mind's eye I am now remembering one particular morning meal in 'Hab School', as we call it, when the twenty or so in my group are in the canteen, sampling a particularly revolting concoction of sweet and sour soy and a mug of synthetic pea soup. I have taken one fork-full of the sweet and sour followed by a sip of the pea soup, then I'm suddenly overcome by a wave of nausea. I jump out of my seat and run for the bathroom, hand over my mouth, leaving my fellow students staring after me in complete surprise.

I spend a full 10 minutes throwing up in the toilet, then wash down my face before coming back to the canteen feeling that all eyes are on me.

"How yer feeling Princess?" Roy Bigley asks me with a grin. He's a large well-muscled jock/jerk who sees me as competition and tries to attract my attention at every opportunity. Of recent times he's resorted to bad-mouthing me behind my back, since he's finally realised he has absolutely no prospect of winning me over.

His remark seems to amuse everyone in the room and I notice a lot of the others are laughing at my expense. I resume my seat and try a seaweed biscuit to settle my stomach feeling everyone's eyes on me.

But the 'Princess' nickname sticks and I subsequently hear people referring to me as 'Princess of the Peas' behind my back, accompanied by more sniggering." I pause to take a sip of my beer helping to deaden my recollection of the revolting synthetic pea soup.

"But from what you've told me that cannot have been the end of it?" Nat says after I had recounted this tale.

"It wasn't simply the nickname. Some of them got up to tricks designed to make bad tasting food taste much worse. One meal time I sampled a synthetic tomato soup, or that was what it was called on the sign next to the urn. I'm guessing some in my group had deliberately concocted a mixture of peas and red coloured sauce, then boiled off some of the liquid to concentrate it further. That prank must have taken some planning and most of the group would have been briefed to avoid trying it themselves. So I was the only one to be caught. It had a foul taste, cross between sugar and mud. It made me gag. I had to stop eating and run for the bathroom yet again, where I couldn't stop puking and suffered acute diarrhoea soon after."

"Didn't you suspect that this was a deliberate test by your selectors to check out your sensitivity, rather than a malicious trick by others in your group?"

"Yes that did cross my mind. I never got to the bottom of it. Whether it was intentional or not, it had the effect of ruining my chances for taking part in the first habitat mission. A week or two after these episodes I was called in to go over what had been going on. They asked me about my nickname, although I'm sure they'd worked it out or had it explained that I was now generally known as 'The Princess of the Peas'."

Nat surprises me by reaching out and holding my hand in a gesture of sympathy, as I dab my eyes. I'm touched but don't hang on to him for too long. He's turning out to be a lot more sensitive than I'd imagined.

I pull myself together and continue with my story. "If I hadn't been de-selected, I may have resigned anyway. I was missing Marg, my former partner, and had never quite reconciled myself to the fact that my journey to Mars would absolutely be the end of our relationship."

I tell Nat this deliberately so he'll understand I'm gay, which in my case doesn't entirely rule me out from being attracted to certain types of men. He displays no reaction so I'm assuming it comes as no surprise to him, particularly since he must come across all sorts of people behind the bar. He's still listening as I'm pondering what he really thinks about me, and how much more I should reveal. But he's looking more and more interested, so I continue.

"So I was almost at the point of giving in, as I couldn't imagine spending the rest of my life in a colony that would not only be an ongoing struggle with an unimaginably harsh environment, and an equally unrewarding social experience."

"Wow that's strange, not what I would have expected. From what you've told me you're not the sort of person who'd give up that easily?"

"You're right. I didn't give up that easily, partly because I did also suspect I might have been subjected to a deliberate test for character or physiological negatives. So I refused to give up and begged them to give me a second chance. To my surprise they agreed to set up some special allergy and taste tests, to work out what it was that was producing my strong negative reactions."

"You mean they didn't believe you really deserved such a nickname?"

"Everyone by now was still calling me 'Princess', and it looked like I was stuck with that. But you know what?" Nat shakes his head, obviously having no idea of my next revelation.

I pause for a long moment, to make sure I have his attention.

"I shouldn't be telling you this. I want you to promise, absolutely, you will not reveal this to anyone."

"Sure of course ... what's the big secret?"

"I actually *am* a princess." I say, taking a last sip of my drink.

Nat has a strange expression on his face, and I cannot decide whether he's about to laugh or he's thinking I'm crazy, needing to be humoured. "You've got to be kidding," he says softly.

"No I'm not joking. You've heard of Princess Josefine of Denmark?"

"Yes everybody has. You're not telling me you're related?"

Ignoring the sarcasm in his voice, I continue with my explanation.

"Not exactly. We were born in the same hospital, at exactly the same time, and I only recently discovered that there must have been a mix up. I'm actually the Royal. Josefine's the commoner. We have similar blonde hair and yes we are both female but that's where the resemblance ends."

"So how did you work out there was a mix up, and more to the point, why should I believe this. It all sounds just too fantastic!" Nat is beginning to sound like he is losing patience.

"Yes I can understand you saying that. I wouldn't have believed it myself were it not for the scientific evidence the selectors for the Mars Mission produced. You see Josefine's mother, maternal grandmother, and previous female generations of her line of descent, carry a particular genetic characteristic. It causes an acute allergy to a mixture of pea protein and a special preservative that was developed in Denmark during the 1950s. A local food company marketed a product by the name of 'Pea Hamper' in English. It became famous overnight when it was sampled by members of the Royal Family as a PR stunt. It caused Josefine's great great grand-mother to spend a day or two in hospital with food poisoning. Fortunately it wasn't fatal, but has been well documented since that episode. Unfortunately the use of this preservative became very common even outside Denmark."

"That seems strange given the risk of causing such an allergic reaction?"

"It is extremely rare, much less common than the reaction peanuts can cause, for example. Anyway, the

Mission selectors discovered that I'm carrying the exact rare gene that the Royal Family members have. That led to them to investigating me further. They were aware that Denmark was the country of my birth and found out that I was born at the same time and location as Princess Josefine. But my parents were not alive to confirm any of that, and after going through documents they left behind, found nothing to shed any light on what might have happened. I do of course know that I was born in Denmark, was adopted out and migrated with my parents to Australia. We arrived here in 2030."

"Well what effect did all this have on your selectors?"

"Predictable ones. They were concerned about the bad publicity should it become more widely known, possibly a liability for the whole mission. So in return for my signing a no-sunset confidentiality agreement, I received a generous payout for my silence, the amount of which I am not allowed to disclose to anyone."

"So why are you telling me this!"

"I don't know really. I need to talk to someone and am hoping I can trust you?" Nat stares at me as I say this. It's me pressing his hand this time, to make sure that he's listening and agrees.

"If you decided to blab to someone, I will deny everything I've told you of course."

I wasn't really worried, even though such a story might tempt an aspiring journalist, and he really didn't seem the type to betray a trust.

5 YEARS LATER

Before leaving Australia I had almost succeeded in turning my friendship with Nat into an enduring relationship. I'd come to realise that he and I have a lot in common, despite the fact I'd been in a gay relationship before him. Then work opportunities intervened. I was offered a senior PR role with Micro Comms, and forced to make the difficult decision to move to the United States, once again by myself.

But our lives seemed to be destined to intersect once more when I was seconded to their London Office, and shortly discovered that Nat was also scheduled to visit Europe via London for his own work reasons.

He just called me out of the blue, and three days later we're seated in the bar of the London Journalist's Association. Nat is still looking as youthful as when I last saw him. Maybe there are a couple more wrinkles on his forehead but he seems essentially the same person. I'm hoping to find more about what he's up to.

After the initial chit chat Nat says something I would never have expected: "I have managed to wangle an invitation to a dinner in Copenhagen where Princess Josefine is guest of honour. I really want to go but I'd love you to come with me and we can maybe delve further into that question which I know is so important to you."

I feel gob-smacked. "How did you manage to score such an honour?"

"Well there's to be an official Garden Party in honour of Princess Josefine's engagement to ..." He'd momentarily forgotten her suitor's name.

"Bernard Osman," I filled it in for him. "But how did you manage the invitation?"

"The Australian Consul there happens to be an old school friend, and he wangled the invitation for me, it is a 'plus one invite', so I would love you to come along with me."

"Have you managed to see Princess Josefine the other times you have been to Copenhagen?" I asked

"No, only on holo-casts. Apart from her blonde hair, she bears little or no resemblance to you as you've no doubt checked. So I'd really like to meet her in the flesh, and I imagine you would, wouldn't you?"

"I'm not at all sure about this. I'm terrified of meeting someone who's holding royal status that belongs to me."

"I think it's time for you to lay the ghost don't you?"

What could I say other than to nod my head?

« »

The 'real princess' doesn't have much to say to me when we're introduced, except for the standard pre-lunch chit chat. We're interrupted by a call to be seated. It's a formal affair with a massive dining table holding at least fifty guests. There is a printed menu and waiters are standing at attention behind us dressed in formal livery. It's an impressive occasion and I have no idea about protocol, except I suppose that everybody must wait until the Princess starts eating.

I've noticed that they've seated Nat right next to her (his friend in the Embassy must have some real pull!) I'm relegated to half way down the table between two men neither of whom speak English fluently. One's from Russia the other from Indonesia.

I have nearly given up trying to make conversation with them, and in any case I've been distracted reading the menu which, much to my surprise, lists pea soup as the entree. I'm wondering whether my theory about Josefine is correct and she will not be affected by the soup, since it's me who suffers the allergy to pea soup and have the royal gene. I'm keenly watching as she absentmindedly dips her spoon into the soup and takes a sip, while deep in discussion with Nat on her right. I am fascinated to see her face immediately starting to twitch.

Rodney Jensen

She seems to have lost interest in conversation. Then suddenly, she clutches a hand to her mouth, rises to her feet and rushes out of the room, to everyone's amazement. There's a buzz of stunned conversation.

Shortly afterwards, a uniformed flunky makes an announcement in suitably solemn tones that the remaining courses are to be suspended out of respect for Her Majesty and we're invited to check out the landscaped gardens before leaving. As I'm passing through the door I hear a loud crash and watch a waiter rush over to pick up a plate that has been knocked from the head of the table to the floor and broken into pieces.

Soon after that Nat joins me in the garden. "Let's get out of here. I don't want to hang around, I'll explain later," he mutters, and we join the line of departing guests in animated discussion.

Nat tells me that he has to make a dash for his office to file a story about the Princess and we agree to meet up the coming weekend in London as I have a number of appointments banking up for my attention.

« »

The weekend is here, and at the moment I'm living in Knightsbridge in a small flat up a lot of stairs so I've suggested that we meet in Hyde Park on Sunday afternoon if the weather's nice. Nat arrives on time, rugged up in a heavy coat despite it being June. He's looking extremely smug like he's made a scoop or won a lottery.

"You've discovered something haven't you?"

Nat's response is to pull out a piece of paper and hand it to me. It's a formally printed document headed DNA Report. I read what it has to say, finding it difficult to take in. "It says that the two samples of DNA you supplied are confirmed as from sisters. Relating to your additional question about the pea hamper gene, both samples have it."

"That's right," he replies. "Yours is one of the samples. The other is from Princess Josefine."

"However did you get that?"

"Yours was easy. It was on the camera you gave me when we last saw each other in Sydney. Josefine's wasn't quite as simple. I had to create a diversion at the banquet and while everyone was focused on the waiter rushing over to clear up the broken plate, I snaffled the spoon that Princess Josefine was using to eat her soup. I don't suppose it will be missed. There must be many others of exactly the same pattern." He pauses then remembers something else.

"By the way, in Copenhagen the news reported that Princess Josefine of Denmark was in hospital suffering from food poisoning."

Nat is watching me closely as he tells me this, but I simply nod.

"Before I say anything more, I have a question for you," he says staring at me as if he's an eminent barrister about to hammer a witness.

"Ask away …" I'm feeling wary because perhaps he's spotted something else.

"How come you're not surprised about the effect of that soup on Josefine, Celine?"

"What do you mean?"

"You know perfectly well what I mean. You're supposed to be the one that's allergic to peas, not Josefine!"

"OK smarty pants. You've caught me out in a little fib. But actually most of what I told you is true."

Rodney Jensen

"Well what part of it isn't—and if you were fibbing why should I believe anything you've told me!"

"Calm down," I say, not sounding particularly calm myself. "I think the truth is that Josefine and I are actually non-identical twins, but as your report shows, we both do have the pea hamper gene."

"So why did you imply that you were unrelated babies both born at the same time?"

"It was a hope really," I say. "I thought a mix up was the better thing to believe than the twin possibility. If we had been twins why would our parents have decided to give me away for adoption? That I have never been able to understand, and there is nothing in my adoptive parents papers to explain it. But now you've come up with what seems like more persuasive evidence, I will have to accept the facts."

"Maybe you will," He says to me in a quiet voice. "You're not looking at all happy?"

"No of course I'm not. I would have far preferred to have been an accidental mix-up than a deliberate choice made by my biological parents. And I don't suppose I am ever going to get to the bottom of it."

"If it were me I would be eternally grateful not to be encumbered by royalty. Think of the freedom you have that you never would have had otherwise," Nat says with his usual common sense approach.

"You know what? I think you're right. The dream of being the real princess would almost certainly turn out to be a nightmare. Thank you for digging up the truth. I'd like you to help me get very drunk tonight, now I'm faced with something that could massively affect my future if I chose to pursue it."

Epilogue

I'm standing next to Nat watching the holo feed from Habitat I. It's the completion of a dream to gain the toehold on Mars I took part in some years ago. We watch as Habitat's view of *"Sjernedestinationer"* our very own starship comes onto the screen. We are docking with the Mars Terminus Satellite and will use the 'nanovator', a passenger gondola that is tethered to a very long cable of super-carbon fibre.

Shortly, I will be heading down to the surface of Mars for a welcoming party and farewell from the first colonists. Nat has decided to stay behind in charge of our ship, making sure everything is as it should be for our larger mission, a journey to explore one of Earth's nearest and presumed habitable exo-planets.

I am reflecting on how our fortunes have turned after I finally changed my mind and decided to threaten a legal suit against both the Danish Government and the Royal Family. My legitimate claim to be the twin sister of Princess Josefine inevitably succeeded once it was realised how unjustly I had been treated at birth, and the bad publicity for the Royal Family if the details of my claim were leaked. So I became Princess Celine, and as my consort, Nat has become The Honourable Nathaniel Pitt, despite my sense of the absurdity of it all.

Far from sitting back luxuriating in my new status, I've been very busy recommending important reforms to the Denmark economy. With my considerable interest in space exploration I've spearheaded the formation of a new space bureau. My favourite program has been the development of this spaceship capable of travelling to the stars.

One day I think to myself, we might be able to return to Earth centuries later by Earth time and check out

Rodney Jensen

whether the intended program of Mars terraforming, to create a breathable atmosphere and warmer climatic conditions has been a success.

« »

Reference for Tale 10

This story is based on the well-known Andersen tale, "The Real Princess" in which a Prince wishes to find a real Princess to marry, and after scouring candidates far and wide, remains un-satisfied with any of them.

On the night of a tempest over the palace, the old King discovers a young woman knocking at the door requesting shelter for the night. The Queen decides to test the girl's claim to be a Princess by sending her to bed on which she has placed a little pea, covered by twenty mattresses and twenty featherbeds over the mattresses.

The next morning the girl's claims of spending a restless night and hurting so much she is black and blue from lying on something hard under her, convinces everyone that she is the real Princess and a suitable partner for the Prince.

In this re-imagined story, the proof that Celine is actually a twin sister to Princess Josefine of Denmark turns on the fact that both share an acute allergy to a particular brand of Danish pea soup.

« »

Rodney Jensen

Please review this anthology

I hope that you enjoyed 'Tales for the Time Traveller'. I would appreciate it if you could spare a few moments to write a sentence or two in review. This helps other readers to decide if it is something they might also enjoy, and also it very much helps me as an author.

Please put a review where you purchased the book or on my website using the link below:

Review TforTTT[2]

« »

Be one of the first to read the second volume of the Covert Trilogy

In 'Covert Citadel', you will learn how arch rivals of the Nest, the 'Aggressives', take advantage of the pandemic weakened population of Earth to attempt global conquest of the planet.

Sign up to Rodney Jensen Books Mailing List

Subscribe [3]

…. and I will let you know as soon as it is available.

---

[2] https://rodneyjensenbooks.com/review-tales-time-traveller/
[3] https://www.subscribepage.com/y4a2w9_copy2

Rodney Jensen

Acknowledgments

My partner Liz McCarthy has provided ongoing inspiration and support in the development of this anthology, informing many of my ideas and conversations, patiently editing and proofing successive drafts leading to this final version.

I also owe a great deal to Chloe Barber Hancock who has injected structural suggestions and insight into the beta version.

Graphic designer Trina Ding's contribution includes the imaginative cover and separate story images.

I also must acknowledge thoughts and suggestions of fellow members of the Northern Beaches Writers' Group in Sydney and founder Zena Shapter for ongoing encouragement for this and other published short stories.

Historic images included at the end of each chapter in this book are the work of the notable British artist Rex Whistler illustrating "Fairy Tales and Legends" by Hans Andersen in an edition first published in 1935 by Cobden Sanderson Ltd in London. Whistler the son of an architect and real estate agent was tragically killed in action on his first day of active service with a tank corps in Normandy in 1944 towards the end of World War II. The image illustrating Cinderella and her ugly sisters is by illustrator Charles Folkard contained in a 1949 edition of Grimms' Fairy Tales published by JM Dent and Sons Ltd.

About the author

Rodney Jensen is a speculative fiction writer focused on how current trends will shape the near future. The early version of Covert Messages was written several years before the COVID 19 pandemic. It has been interesting to find that many of his original speculations about global pandemics have proven to be accurate and required only minor revisions in light of recent actual events.

Other aspects of his speculative fiction are influenced by his environmental background, experience as an urban designer and passion for renewable energy. Similarly his interests in artificial intelligence, the search for extra-terrestrial intelligence (SETI) and new theories of the cosmos have been important inspirations.

He is fascinated by the notion of a cosmic-scale artificial intelligence network waiting for the appropriate time to make first contact with humankind. Rodney hopes that within his own lifetime the discovery of extra-terrestrial intelligence will overturn the generally held belief that our intelligent species is alone in the cosmos.

Other Books by Rodney Jensen

Find out more about Rodney, these and other books at his website: http://www.rodneyjensenbooks.com/

What reviewers have said about Rodney Jensen's books ...

"If you enjoy futuristic science fiction and extra-terrestrial experiences, this [Covert Messages] is the book for you. The references to the past COVID-19 pandemic of 2020 are chilling and force you to consider our own current situation, as the more serious pandemic of 2035 unfolds in the book. Rodney Jensen utilises his knowledge of Australian geography as he weaves a sombre tale, but includes the more positive romance or two as well. Also, I found the antics and behaviour of the dog Marshall as he is unknowingly manipulated by the extra-terrestrials quite delightful." Elizabeth Saadeh

« »

"Much thought, imagination and care has gone into this chilling and provocative novel. It ['Covert Citadel'] is a post -pandemic dystopian vision set in the out-back wastes of New South Wales and its devastated towns where a courageous few eke out a sparse existence. A young woman, Sam Mitchell provides hope, rallying a brave band of technologically adept survivors who stand up to the threat of a sinister and destructive alien power." Jenny Towndrow.

« »

"The novel [now entitled 'Covert State'] is a well-paced traditional detective story set in the near future with a concealed sci-fi twist. The characters are engaging, skilfully presented as people you may already know. It takes you on a journey through Adelaide and its Hills, Sydney and the enigma that is Indonesia and its stormy relationship with Australia. An easy to read and most enjoyable Australian crime novel." Andy McGee.

Rodney Jensen

Extract from 'Covert Messages'

Covert Messages is the first volume of Rodney Jensen's **Covert Trilogy** is widely available. Here is the Prologue for you to enjoy:

« »

As the bio-scientists were quietly going about their experiments in the top security lab, they were jolted into urgent escape mode by the penetrating and pulsating rasp of an emergency siren. In their anxiety to retreat the research staff in full PPE (Personal Protective Equipment) had torn off the air hoses tying them to their work stations and run to the isolation airlock separating their lab from other parts of the complex.

Each knew from their training they had a maximum of thirty seconds to do this before the airlock door would be sealed. It had been drilled into them that if anyone missed the door sealing there could be no recovery until the lab had been fully cleared—in all likelihood leaving that person fatally exposed to contamination.

The year was 1980—a time when the Cold War between the Soviet Union and the West was at its height and many defense experts on both sides feared the onset of World War III.

In a part of the world remote from Moscow, but nevertheless vulnerable to invasion along its northern coastline, researchers were quietly investigating chemical and bio-agents in a top-secret installation hidden beneath the Garden Island Naval Base in the heart of Sydney, Australia. This was in spite of the universally accepted world convention prohibiting the use of bio-agents in warfare.

Rodney Jensen

The laboratories were laid out at different levels in the complex with increasing protection measures against accidental infection. The biological agents were isolated from the working areas by purpose-designed bio-cabinets equipped with hand access ports, a system the risk analysts were confident provided 99.9% security for all those working in the lab, or anyone in the wider locality.

One winter morning their optimism was to be shattered.

« »

That same morning, Craig Wilkinson, a young biologist unaware of the critical situation at his workplace, was making his way to the installation from Circular Quay via the Botanic Gardens. He noticed a strange odor the moment he reached the middle of the Gardens. As he turned at a bend in the pathway, the strange smell was growing by the second, and a menacing cloud of black smoke was wafting his way. If he had been thinking more clearly he might have turned back and taken a different route to work, but as it was he was running late and decided to press on, pulling a handkerchief to his nose.

Passing the grove of tall Port Jackson fig trees close to the south-eastern entrance, a strange scene was unfolding. Men wearing protective gloves and face masks were sweeping up small furry objects and piling them into several forty-four gallon drums. They had obviously used kerosene as an accelerant and the putrid fumes made his eyes smart and his stomach heave.

As he got closer to one of the drums he could see that the men were incinerating dead fruit bats. Craig's curiosity was immediately piqued and, despite his nausea, he bent over one of the bats, noticing that its mouth was clamped shut in a death's grimace with red froth oozing from between its teeth. Unable to curb his overwhelming curiosity, he carefully touched the froth with the index finger of his left hand and sniffed, recoiling from the quite unfamiliar and powerful odor.

"I wouldn't touch that if I was you, mate!" yelled one of the workmen, his voice muffled by the face mask he was wearing.

"What happened to them?" he asked, curious to know whether the bats had been deliberately poisoned.

"Haven't a clue, mate. Something happened to them last night. We're burning the lot to reduce the risk of whatever it is from spreading to the other colonies."

« »

Within the administration wing of the installation an urgent meeting had been convened. The staff were of mixed ages, and the man who was chairing the meeting looked to be in his mid-fifties. His Australian accent was modulated by a slight twang, suggesting he had spent some career time in the United States. The atmosphere of the meeting was electric.

"I'm not pointing the finger," he said, despite the tone of his voice indicating otherwise, "but what I do require is an honest and objective assessment of the potential risks we are facing. Just how much HRNX-0 has escaped and how it happened—that's what I'd like to know."

"It seems that one of the maintenance team forgot to put back one of the filter panels in the exhaust system. Fortunately, the escape monitor triggered and the ventilation system was shut off immediately," said James, an intent and conservatively dressed young engineer. He punctuated his words with a flapping hand, making a turning motion like he was shutting off a valve.

Rodney Jensen

"That's not all I asked, James," said the Chair. "Just how much got out?"

The young man's eyes involuntarily darted sideways as he tried to formulate a satisfactory answer. "We can't be sure, sir, but we estimate as much as ten grams may have escaped in the worst case scenario."

"In the *worst case scenario*," the Chair mimicked him angrily, "what impact is that likely to have on the thousands of people who are living and working near here?"

"I doubt that anyone's been able to make that assessment yet," said Craig, who had just joined the meeting from his encounter in the park, "but there is something that *is* potentially serious." His face was pallid and he was sipping from a glass of water with a visible tremor in his hand.

"Let us be the judge of that, Craig," said the Chair, quietly, in an authoritative tone.

"I usually walk through the Botanic Gardens on my way to work. This morning something was going on that didn't make sense. Some of the workmen were burning bats. There were piles of them. I checked one—not a pretty sight—looked like it had hemorrhaged and the blood had a very strange smell. I don't think those guys had any idea what it was and claimed they were burning them as a precaution against it spreading. If I'd known about this leak I would have been telling them to get the hell out of there, and I suppose…"

"Yep, we get the picture!" said the Chair without waiting for him to finish, and turned to the PA who was sitting next to him taking notes. "Cheryl, I want you to get in touch with the head of the Botanic Gardens, tell whoever it is that the men must stop burning the dead bats immediately, and get in here without delay. Stress that it's absolutely urgent and can't wait."

Craig's message and the Chair's reaction galvanized the meeting. No one knew where to look. Everyone was wondering whether they had somehow been responsible. One or two were jotting meaningless words on their scratchpads, unwilling to confront the worst possible scenario.

"We've got to nip this in the bud before news spreads, and put a clamp on anyone who has heard or seen what Craig has reported," the Chair continued. He turned back to his PA, who was looking hesitant. "What are you waiting for, Cheryl? Get on with it. Immediately!"

As she dashed out to do her boss's bidding, he closed the meeting, stressing, "I want everyone to stop what they've been doing and investigate all possible leads; doctors, hospitals, clinics, any place where someone who's been infected might have gone—leave no stone unturned. I cannot stress the absolute necessity: not a word of this gets out. It's a matter of utmost national security—your reports to me by this evening."

Craig had scrambled to his feet, clutching his stomach, and rushed towards the door. But he never made it, collapsing to the floor and doubling up in pain. Others jumped to assist, but by the time they had reached him he was already dead; eyes wide, and face contorted, his mouth frothing like the bats.

Absolute pandemonium erupted, some members of the meeting wringing their hands while staring helplessly at the body, others backing away in terror, but most realizing that their path to door was blocked were paralyzed in fright.

The fact that Craig was lying directly across the entrance was fortuitous. The Chair kept his head realizing that it would be catastrophic for a roomful of infected staff to make a run for anywhere outside the building. He picked up his communicator and called security ordering them to send someone to guard their entrance, notify their special medical emergency contacts and prevent anyone leaving the building.

The Chair was honest enough to realize his response was too little too late. He and his minions now contemplated the possibility of mass fatalities in the immediate vicinity of their research installation. But in one sense they were lucky. No information of what had occurred ever leaked into the public domain, and apart from Craig, there were no other recorded infections at that time.

'Covert Messages' is available now as an eBook and paperback at most online retailers including:

Amazon

Book Depository

Barnes and Noble

Fishpond

…and many more

Already read it? Then be one of the first to read the second volume of the Covert Trilogy

In 'Covert Citadel', you will learn how arch rivals of the Nest, the 'Aggressives', take advantage of the pandemic weakened population of Earth to attempt global conquest of the planet.

Sign up to

RodneyJensenBooks Mailing List[4]

…. and I will let you know as soon as it is available.

---

[4] https://www.subscribepage.com/y4a2w9_copy2